The Gho

Bald Head
Island

A REUNION OF COLLEGE
FRIENDS TURNS DEADLY

A Perfect Beach Novel

Jeremy Hutchinson, J.D.

NEWMAN SPRINGS PUBLISHING
320 Broad Street
Red Bank, NJ 07701

First originally published by Newman Springs Publishing 2022

ISBN 978-1-68498-610-1 (Paperback)
ISBN 979-8-88763-132-5 (Hardcover)
ISBN 978-1-68498-611-8 (Digital)

Printed in the United States of America

BALD HEAD ISLAND
North Carolina

CHAPTER 1

Dr. Theron Mason

Sunday—

I had been looking forward to this trip for some time. If I was being honest, I had been anticipating this trip since I graduated college in 2004, which was the last time I had seen Sophie. It was June 23, 2020—Bald Head Island was hosting the annual Pirate Invasion. The Pirate Invasion is a popular festival. The island welcomes tourists who adorn themselves in pirate garb, decorate their sailboats and sloops with skull and crossbones flags, pack their bikinis, and load up with enough rum to last a long weekend.

On this day, I was maneuvering my boat up the Carolina Coast to reunite at the Pirate Invasion with five of my old college friends from Furman University. Furman is a small liberal arts college in Greenville, South Carolina. Of the six friends, I had always been the serious one. They would probably label me the aloof one of the group. I don't view myself as aloof; I just had to study more than the rest of them. My friends never appreciated how hard it was to become a doctor—it meant sacrificing meaningless hours of fun with my friends so that I could remain hidden away in the university's Sanders Science Library. The science library only had one study room comprised of a table, a chair, and an electrical outlet. Students had to reserve the study room, and there was much competition for reservations. If I did manage to secure a reservation, I couldn't cancel the reservation to spend a night at the Gaslight Bar and Lounge, which was one of our crew's favorite hangout spots.

At least my sacrifices during college had paid off. I was now a relatively successful bariatric surgeon. I still operated in the Greenville/Spartanburg area. Because of med school and work responsibilities, I never found the time to date anyone—at least not seriously. I was the only one of my friends who had never married. I know that it was shallow of me, but I was anxious to show my old college friends how successful I was. I wouldn't rub my wealth in their face. I wouldn't have to. After all, it was my sailboat/yacht that we would be hanging out on all week. And what a boat she was—an Oyster 885 that I had named *Nomism's*. *Nomism* is a Greek word meaning strict adherence to moral law. I thought that, since my "rule following" had put me in a position to buy this boat, *Nomism's* would be a good name for her. There is a secondary reason that I chose that name, but that reason is personal. I would prefer to keep my second reason private, at least for the time being.

The *Nomism's* was a ninety foot luxury cruising yacht with five guest cabins and the draft of 3.1 meters. My boat was large enough to sleep all my old college friends and their significant others. There was a deck on the stern of the boat with a bar and sitting area. The large saloon could easily entertain twelve people. The dining room connected the large saloon with the galley. The small saloon had another bar and poker table. On the bow of the boat was an out-door kitchen / bar-and-lounge area. The promenade deck primarily consisted of the helm, which was located within the bridge. It was a beautiful boat—my pride and joy.

My thoughts were interrupted when the sail began to luff. My boat was designed to be operated by a small crew. However, since I would be gone for a week, my "crew" consisted of Tommy—Tommy was a sixteen-year-old boy who lived with an alcoholic mother. Tommy had a mop of sandy-blond hair and a lean frame. He would someday be a strapping young man, but at this stage in his development, he still looked like he was twelve years old. Tommy spends most of his time at the Myrtle Beach docks doing odd jobs. When I asked him if he wanted to learn to sail, he jumped at the chance. I paid for Tommy to take sailing lessons, and I invited him to go sailing with me every weekend. Within a few months, Tommy had gained my complete confidence in his sailing abilities. I was hesitant to invite him on the trip, but I knew that I would be drinking with my friends. Someone needed to man the boat.

The *Nomism's* had a large volume hull form with twin rudders, which made the boat very stable and easy to control from the helm. Visibility was excellent from both helm stations, making tricky maneuvers simple even for a one-man crew.

As long as the weather cooperated, I could handle the boat by myself, with Tommy's marginal assistance. Standing at the helm, I adjusted the point of sail, turning the boat away from the wind. There I was at full sail again. I knew that I would have to be more focused as I approached Cape Fear at the tip of Bald Head Island. The Carolina coastline can provide a beautiful distraction. I left Myrtle Beach yesterday morning and had a few more hours before I arrived at the bay in Southport, North Carolina, where I was scheduled to meet my old friends.

The Carolina's coastline is low and flat. The mouths of numerous streams and rivers empty into sounds or the ocean itself. I love watching the water change colors as a river empties itself into the ocean. There is such vibrancy of life as two ecosystems converge into one another. Lighthouses dot the landscape and act in the same way as mile markers on an interstate. I made a point to learn the history of each lighthouse that I pass, but to date, none have intrigued me like the Old Baldy Lighthouse on Bald Head Island. Not only was Old Baldy a beautiful structure with incredible history, but it served a valuable service as it protected unsuspecting sailors from the very dangerous shoals which extended beyond Cape Fear—the tip of Bald Head Island.

I had a few more hours, though, before I encountered the shoals; so I took my shirt off to improve my tan. I looked at my torso. Damn it, I worked out every day. I paid for a trainer. I watched my diet, and yet there was still flab. My physique was acceptable for a man of my age but not acceptable for a man who spent as much energy and money on it as I did. My physique reminded me of that luff sail that I had just fixed. Like the luff sail, my body was functional but looked a little deflated.

My mind wandered to what Sophie would think of my body. Why do I torture myself with such thoughts? She never saw me as anything beyond friends while we were in college; would her recent divorce or my shiny new sailboat really make her see me any differently sixteen years later? Maybe—just maybe. That hope is why I organized this reunion. I wanted an excuse to see Sophie again, and if that meant reuniting with old friends and reliving some old insecurities, then so be it. A chance to be with Sophie was worth it.

CHAPTER 2

Ben Eiler

Why did I agree to do this? Sixteen years ago, I celebrated our graduation night with these friends—that is, everyone but Theron Mason, who said he had to study for the MCAT. That night, I determined that I would never see these people again, and I had honored that decision. My life was good, not great, but decent. Why open old wounds now? I was curious how my friends' lives had turned out, and I guess my curiosity had gotten the best of me. Besides, my wife had been nagging me for years to take her on a beach trip without our eight kids. This trip would let me fulfill her request at a reduced cost since Theron was footing most of the cost of the trip.

What terrified me, though, was that there was so much about my past that my wife didn't know. Surely my old college friends had gained enough maturity to not divulge the deep, dark secrets of our past. After college, I went to Africa for a few years: Kampala, Uganda, to be precise. I don't know if I went to escape my parents' oversight or in a feeble attempt at redemption. I got a job with the United States' Agency for International Development (USAID). I was tasked with teaching local Ugandans the values of capitalism, free trade, and American democracy. It was awful.

I know that it is wrong of me to think this, but I hated Uganda and immediately knew that I had made a huge mistake. Unfortunately I had made a three-year commitment, so I tried to make the best of it. I walked everywhere. I would sometimes walk fifteen miles a day. I embraced the local food. I never realized how many chemicals and preservatives are in Americans' processed food. I ate fresh fruit—and not fruit that you would buy at the local grocery store. I ate mangos, lychee berries, and papaya. If I ate meat, it was meat that I watched be butchered in front of me. I was in the best shape of my life.

I also met my wife, Lauren, in Uganda. Lauren also worked for USAID and had arrived in Uganda only six months before me. Other than Sophie, she was the nicest person that I had ever met. She was cute, nothing like Sophie, but few women could compare to Sophie. Laura was a little overweight but worked hard to minimize the effects of her genetics. Unlike me, she really did care for the people of Uganda and was determined to make a difference in their lives. In fact, she adopted two Ugandan babies who had lost both of their parents to one of the many diseases that plagued the continent of Africa. I thought that she was both crazy and courageously kind. A young single woman adopting two Ugandan babies—insane, right? I can't criticize her decision too much because, two years later, I married Lauren and adopted her two Ugandan children. We then went on to have six children ourselves after we moved to Atlanta.

While I hated my job with USAID, it did provide me with an opportunity to be hired as a vice president of international markets at Coca-Cola. Impressive title, huh? Truth is there are hundreds of vice presidents at Coca-Cola. It's a title that looks impressive on a business card but possesses very little power within the corporate structure. The pay is decent—for an average family of four. But for a family of ten? It doesn't even begin to pay for the lifestyle that I had always imagined for myself.

"What are you thinking about?" Lauren asked.

We had been in our ten-passenger white Ford Transit van for four hours and had another two hours before arriving at South Port, North Carolina.

"I don't know," I said. "I guess I was just thinking about life since college."

Laura always managed to ask insightful questions. She asked me, "Are you worried that your life won't stack up to their lives?"

I should have reacted with more patience, but I didn't. "Well, of course I am worried about the comparisons. Everyone who goes to any reunion is worried about comparing jobs, spouses, incomes, and waistlines."

"Well," Laura smiled and said, "you will at least win the spouse comparison."

With that, she turned her head and began reading her book again.

Lauren was indeed a saint, and I did love her. But after giving birth to six children, she had lost her battle with her genetics. She was still pretty when she tried to be, but most of the time, the mother of eight wore sweatpants and no makeup as she tried to survive her day without falling asleep at the wheel as she drove one of the children to their next practice. Sex? I can't remember the last time we had sex—maybe the last time we went on vacation without the kids? It's so bad that I don't even think about it anymore, at least not with her; and I know she doesn't think about it with me or, I suspect, with anyone else.

This vacation should be a time for Lauren and I to decompress and reconnect. Instead I was afraid that she would hate my old friends or at least hate how I behaved around my old friends. Worst case scenario—she found out about Mexico.

CHAPTER 3

Kelly White

"Raymond, we have to hit the road if we are going to make it to South Point by twelve thirty."

I knew that I was asking a lot of my husband to break away from his job as United States deputy attorney general to spend the week with me and my old college friends seven hours away from DC. On top of that, we had to leave at 4:30 a.m. to be able to get from Georgetown to South Point, North Carolina, to meet Theron at his boat by noon.

Raymond's job obviously kept him very busy. I was hoping that he would say no when I invited him to join us at Bald Head Island. I was shocked that he immediately said, "Yeah, I'll go." My guess is that he only decided to go because he knew that I used to be in love with one of my college friends. Her name was Sophie. Surprised that it was a girl? So was Raymond when I told him about her. The truth is that, while I was indeed in love with Sophie, she rebuffed my attempts to take our friendship to the next level. Her rejection only made me desire her more.

After I discovered that Raymond had an affair with a coworker at the Justice Department, I disclosed to him an exaggerated version of my and Sophie's relationship.

It was a pathetic attempt to hurt Raymond in the same way he had hurt me. It didn't work. Instead of being hurt, he seemed intrigued. He asked me hundreds of questions about Sophie—but not in a way that a jealous spouse would inquire. Instead it seemed like, as I told him about Sophie, he was falling for her as well. I was disturbed by his interest in Sophie and even more disturbed that he jumped at the chance to spend a week away from work to meet Sophie.

I was obviously nervous that Raymond would ask Sophie about our "relationship" and she would tell him the truth. I had often felt unworthy around Raymond, but if he found out that I made up a story about having an affair with a girl, he might leave me. I was also worried that he would attempt to seduce Sophie himself. He was slightly older than Sophie and I, but he did look good for his age. Hell, he looked good for any age. His perfectly managed salt-and-pepper hair, coupled with his toned body, gave him hope with any woman that he encountered. After I caught him having the affair with his coworker, he promised to change, and he had. He now only had affairs with women who worked outside the Justice Department.

When I met Raymond in law school, I was a confident, brash, very attractive aspiring lawyer. For Raymond, I became sexually adventurous. It wasn't my preference to have sex in public or wear costumes to satisfy Raymond's fantasies, but for Raymond, I changed who I was. Not only did I change who I was sexually, but I also gave up my plans to be a lawyer. Raymond was a year older than me, so upon his law school graduation, he moved to Washington, DC, to begin his career at the Justice Department. He insisted that I leave law school and go with him. I still had one year of law school left. I told him that I wouldn't follow him to DC unless we were married and unless I could complete my law school studies once we got settled into DC life.

Raymond gave me a ring and assured me that we would have the wedding the following year. Four years later, we were finally married; I never resumed my law school studies. Raymond always had a reason why I shouldn't go back to law school. Unfortunately none of those reasons were that I had become a mother. The fact that Raymond was unable to have children devastated me, but I think Raymond was happy about it. It seemed to have emboldened his adulterous behavior—one risk associated with that behavior was now eliminated. He seemed relieved.

You would think that, with no children produced in the marriage, it would be easy for me to divorce him. However, in a twisted sort of way, I felt more trapped. If I left Raymond, there was no guarantee that I would find anyone new. Having no children and no prospect for a spouse, I was terrified of growing old alone. Moreover, there were financial considerations at play. Raymond's father was an established trial lawyer. As soon as Raymond passed the bar exam, his father added Raymond as counsel to a large case that was on the verge of settling. Raymond's father joked that this fee was in lieu of any inheritance that Raymond would get. I am convinced that Raymond delayed our wedding until the case settled and he had received his millions of dollars in attorney fees. By waiting, Raymond brought his millions of newfound dollars into the marriage. Hence, I was entitled to none of it if we were ever to divorce.

Raymond's job at the Justice Department paid barely over six figures, which is a good living, but most of it was spent on living expenses. He never wanted to touch the money that he had "earned" in his father's case. Having never worked outside the home (at Raymond's insistence), I didn't even have social security to rely on. He had successfully trapped me in this marriage, and I don't even know why. He didn't love me anymore—if he ever did. Why not let me finish my law school studies, earn my own money, and divorce me? He could then be free to explore every sexual encounter to its fullest without having to be discreet around me. The only explanation for his refusal to execute this commonsense plan was his ego.

As we drove to Bald Head, he was on the phone talking to colleagues about prosecuting people who seemed to be far better human beings than Raymond was.

I thought to myself, *The only way I can financially exit my marriage to this controlling hypocrite is for Raymond to die, in which case I would at least be entitled to his government pension and death benefit.*

CHAPTER 4

Steve Camp

"Fuck me."

I didn't know what to do. I had emailed my pretrial parole officer three times requesting permission to travel to Bald Head Island to attend a reunion with my old college friends. I was scheduled to get on the airplane from New York to Wilmington, North Carolina, in an hour; and my probation officer still had not responded to me. I had recently become aware of the fact that our justice system was impossible to navigate. Eighteen months ago, I, along with my company (Gibraltar Assets, a hedge fund), were indicted for insider trading by the Southern District of New York's US Attorney's Office. I had been indicted for a crime which I believed I was innocent of. I had spent a year prior to my indictment trying to explain to prosecutors how the investment banking business worked and why my actions were standard operating procedure for people in my business. However, prosecutors didn't seem to recognize or more likely didn't care for such nuance and indicted me anyway.

At my arraignment, I pleaded not guilty, and the judge released me on my own recognizance since I'd never hurt anyone—at least not since my college days. My only condition was that I had to get permission from my pretrial parole officer to travel outside New York.

I had been seeking permission to travel to Bald Head for three months, and I couldn't get a response—no email response and no phone call after countless of messages left. I was at a loss as to what to do. Here I stood at the airport having purchased a ticket. Screw it, I was going. I handed my ticket to the gate attendant and boarded the plane. The system made it impossible to follow the rules. If I did commit insider trading, I sure as hell didn't know it. I didn't cheat anyone; I didn't steal from anyone. I always assumed that, if you committed a federal crime, you would know you were doing it. I simply used my knowledge and market insight to make money for my clients—and my family.

Speaking of my family, after my indictment, my wife cleaned out our joint accounts, took my two boys, and moved to Martha's Vineyard to live with her parents. She blocked my phone number on the boy's cell phones, and I received divorce papers a few days later. It had been eighteen months, and I still hadn't spoken to my children. I had lost my Series 7 and Series 63 securities licenses and my business license. I cashed in my 401(k) and was living off the proceeds. However, most of that money was going to pay my attorneys. If anyone needed a vacation, it was me.

I would rather go on vacation with a plus-one rather than by myself. Under my current circumstances, I honestly didn't know if I even wanted to see my old college friends again. I doubt any of them knew that I had been indicted, and I was still debating whether or not I should tell them. I'd cross that bridge when I got there. Right now,

I needed to get the stewardess's attention so I could have a pregame drink. This would be the first of many drinks I planned to have this week. I admit that, since my indictment, I had begun to drink more than I should; but honestly who could blame me?

It may surprise you to know that I had also gotten in the best shape of my life. I wish I could tell you that it was because I had a herculean degree of discipline, but the truth is that I worked out and ran because I was bored. All my Wall Street friends have abandoned me; nobody wanted to swim near a drowning man. It had been tough to accept the realization that I never had any true friends—except for Sophie Simmons.

CHAPTER 5

Freedom Goforth

"Damn it, I missed my flight. I need to text Theron and tell him that I will be arriving on the following flight."

Unfortunately I learned that flying out of Santa Fe, New Mexico, wasn't as easy as it was to fly out of Los Angeles. I hated to text Theron "Turns out the next flight isn't for hours. Do you mind having the boat at the pier this evening? Tell everyone that I am so sorry."

I turned to Weston and said, "Well, how do you want to spend the next six hours?"

I had met Weston Walker a year ago when I auditioned to play a supporting role in his new Netflix series. I got the part though it required some after-hours auditioning. The show was never picked up by Netflix, though, so my search for fame would have to wait. Though Weston acted unprofessional at my audition, it turned out that he was not a terrible guy. He had a beautiful home in Taos, New Mexico, and he seemed determined to redeem himself after our first encounter. I hoped he got along with my old college friends.

I called them friends, and I guess they were as close to friends as I had had in my life. But I felt like they defriended me after I left school before our senior year began. You see, this gorgeous lead singer came to Furman with his band. During one of his songs, he noticed me in the audience and motioned for me and Steve Camp (who was with me that night) to go backstage. After he finished his concert, he came backstage. Steve got the hint quickly enough and excused himself. By the next morning, I had decided to use my student loan money to spend a semester with the lead singer in Los Angeles. Predictably the lead singer met another girl while on tour and broke up with me. The relationship didn't last, but I had made it to Hollywood and was never going to go back to Greenville, South Carolina.

My college friends were not hesitant in expressing their disappointment in me for leaving school before my senior year. I tried to explain to them that my parents, who were first-generation French immigrants, named me Freedom for a reason. My friends viewed me as their obligatory "hippie" friend. Well, you don't get the benefit of having a fun-loving, carefree hippie friend without accepting the unorthodox decisions that fun-loving, carefree hippie friends make. Nobody accepted my explanation except for Sophie Simmons.

I should have been jealous of Sophie. God knows that I had been jealous of many women who couldn't hold a candle to Sophie. Sophie was just too nice. As much as I wanted to resent her, I couldn't help but love her. I don't want to seem conceited, but most people considered me to be an attractive woman. But Sophie? Sophie was naturally beautiful. She was so beautiful that she didn't have to try—she rarely wore any makeup beyond a base and some eyeliner. Her naturally tan skin allowed her to do more with less. Likewise, her athletic build required very little effort to maintain. She was courted by most every man who met her, even men who were clearly not in her league. Her kindness and ability to connect with anyone led most men (and women) to believe that she was flirting with them when she was, in fact, only making conversation.

Sophie was the link that had brought all of us friends together. Each of us were first friends with Sophie. She introduced us to each other. Sophie was the type of person whom everyone believed was their best friend. She had a way of making each person feel like they were the most important person in her life. Understand this was not her attempt to manipulate anyone. Sophie was genuinely kind and caring, which I suspected was what led her to become a social worker in Pensacola, Florida.

CHAPTER 6

Sophie Simmons

I had just finished riding my Peloton bike and was scrambling to leave on time. I should have packed last night, but I had an emergency phone call from one of my clients. Shay was a fourteen-year-old girl who had been molested by her mother's boyfriend for years. I managed to get her placed into a foster home while the boyfriend awaited trial. Unfortunately Shay hated her foster family and ran away. She called me from a truck stop in Chattanooga, Tennessee. I managed to convince her to give her foster family another chance, but I then had to drive to Chattanooga through the night to collect her and return her to her foster home. I was operating on two hours of sleep.

Maybe I should call Theron and tell him that I couldn't make the trip. I had missed my old college friends, but I was also a bit angry at them. How could they all just go on with their lives after that fateful day in Mexico? They acted like nothing happened. I wish that I could compartmentalize as well as they had. My guilt led me to become a social worker—I guess as a sort of a penance. My struggle with guilt was also the primary reason for my divorce last year. I believe that there should be no secrets in a marriage, but I had promised my college friends that I would keep this secret to my grave. My ex-husband was a perfectly nice man. He was a dentist who showed me his love by giving me an unlimited credit card.

Nobody could object to such a generous gesture, but that was the only display of affection that he showed me. He worked constantly; he and I had nothing in common. We didn't enjoy each other's company…though we never fought. We respected each other but didn't love each other. Last year, I told him that, for both of our sakes, we should stop trying to act like we had a good marriage. I told him that I wanted children but that I didn't want children with him, not because he would be a poor father, but because our kids would be raised in a loveless household.

He nodded and said he agreed completely. He told me that he would pay for a lawyer to draw up the divorce papers but that I would receive no other support from him. I nodded and said that I didn't want any of his money. I handed him his credit card and moved into a one-bedroom apartment the following day. The last I heard, he was dating one of his dental hygienists. I wish the best for him, and I hope he found the happiness that I could never provide him. While I didn't think the marriage would have worked in the best of circumstances, I knew that my decision to keep the secret from him had to be a contributing factor to our permanent distance.

I was currently dating a great guy. Jed Cummins was an attorney who went through a nasty divorce three years ago. He was a criminal defense attorney but also handled some adoptions, which was how I met him.

Jed was a good-looking guy but had put on a few pounds since his law school days. He shaved his head when his hairline began to recede and looked better bald than he did in the pictures that I'd seen of him with a full head of hair. He was a bit of a bully boy. He played linebacker at Vanderbilt University, and he still lifted weights but did not adhere to a very disciplined diet. I kind of like that about him, though. He was a guy's guy. He was a master chef on the grill. He still loved college football, particularly the Southeastern Conference (SEC). He drank scotch. He smoked cigars when he was with his buddies. He was smart and funny. Everyone who knew him loved him—including me.

I asked him to come with me on this trip; but he had promised his ten-year-old daughter, Claire, that he would take her to a volleyball tournament in Orlando. He was a great dad though his ex-wife did everything she could do to sabotage his relationship with his daughter. So I was on my own this week and very stressed.

I called Jed on my way out of town.

"Hey, baby," he answered.

I began to cry.

"Sophie, what's wrong?" he asked.

"I have no idea, Jed. I wish you were coming with me. I am stressed about seeing my old friends again, and I am exhausted from my late-night escapade to Chattanooga."

Jed was used to my occasional breakdowns, and most of the time, he handled them perfectly. I couldn't blame him for getting frustrated periodically—his occasional frustration with me was not because I was crying. He was frustrated because he didn't know what the cause was for my sudden tears. I wish so bad that I could tell him about Mexico. I truly believe that Jed would understand and love me anyway. I had needed to tell someone, anyone, for sixteen years. Jed would be the perfect person to tell. But first I needed to tell my friends that I was going to tell Jed. Not that I expected to receive their permission, but I figured that I owed them an opportunity to talk me out of it.

"Sophie, if you don't want to go to your Bald Head Island reunion, come to Orlando with Claire and me," Jed offered.

I pulled myself together and thanked him for the offer. I told him that I felt obligated, after sixteen years, to see my college friends—even if it stressed me out.

After a long silence, he said, "Sophie, if Claire's team is eliminated from the tournament early, I will take her to my parents' house for the remainder of the week and come to Bald Head, if you want me to."

"Oh my gosh, Jed, of course I want you to. That would be so amazing. Thank you so much."

Jed responded, "Don't thank me. That would suggest that I am doing you a favor when, in fact, spending a few days on a sun-drenched boat deck off the coast of a beautiful island with you in a bikini is not a sacrifice on my part. In fact, it is an act of utter selfishness."

I blushed and laughed a flirtatious laugh. "Jed," I said, "you are my best friend."

CHAPTER 7

The Reunion

"Dr. Mason, someone is coming up the dock."

Dr. Mason came running onto the deck. "Thank you, Tommy." Dr. Mason suddenly stopped in his tracks and continued talking to me, or maybe he was talking to himself, "Of course, Sophie is the first one here. She always believed being late was the equivalent of theft. Your tardiness stole time from the people that you were scheduled to meet."

I didn't know how to respond, so I didn't. I was mesmerized by Dr. Mason's reaction to seeing this Sophie lady. His face had turned beet red, and I think he was trembling a little bit. I had never seen Dr. Mason like this before. As the lady approached, I began to understand why Dr. Mason was acting so strange. Damn, this Sophie lady was smoking hot. OMG, she had long brown hair with slight curls that bounced as she walked. She was wearing a short white sundress that exposed legs that were tanned, tight, and, well, perfect. She was showing enough cleavage to be sexy but not enough to be slutty, ya know? The sun was shining through her white sundress, exposing the silhouette of very well-maintained body.

"Theron!" she yelled.

She began running toward Dr. Mason. Her boobs were bouncing as she ran. This was going to be a much better trip than I had imagined—and a hell of a lot better than summer school. I had never been more jealous of Dr. Mason than when Sophie jumped into his arms and hugged him. The back of her already-short dress scooted up even further, draping over her hot ass and exposing perfect hamstrings. I couldn't stop staring at her, and Dr. Mason couldn't speak. While I was jealous of him for getting to hug this hottie, I also felt embarrassed for him. He was like I was at the freshman dance with Abby—just a nervous wreck. Dr. Mason clearly had the hots for Sophie, as did I.

After an awkward silence, Dr. Mason finally said, "Sophie, I want you to meet my second mate, Tommy."

I stuck out my hand to shake hers.

She said, "Second mate? That's a very impressive title for such a young man. You must be very good with boats?"

I didn't like that she called me a young man, but now it was my turn to not be able to speak.

"Yes, ma'am" was all I could muster.

Sophie then commented on the boat. "Theron, this boat is incredible. You have done very well for yourself," she said with a hint of flirtation.

I think Dr. Mason blushed, but his face was already so red it was hard to tell.

Sophie then asked us if she could get a tour.

Dr. Mason said, "Of course."

He put his hand on the small of her back and began to escort her into the concourse of the boat.

Just then, the owner of the marina yelled, "Dr. Mason, I need to get a credit card from you and any food or liquor requests that you may have!"

I took my opportunity. "I'll give you a tour, Ms. Sophie."

That was the first time that I had ever seen Dr. Mason glare at me with anger. I didn't care. Sophie agreed, and we began our tour. She spent much of the tour asking me about my life, my mom, and my school. Within twenty minutes, she knew more about me than Dr. Mason knew about me after spending months together.

She was also very impressed with the boat. "Tommy, how does the boat smell so good? It doesn't matter what room we enter. The scent always reminds me of the lobby at the Encore Hotel in Las Vegas. It's a mix of vanilla with some lavender."

I explained to Ms. Sophie that there was an internal system that emitted a fragrance every three minutes throughout the boat. She was very impressed with this small feature.

I loved how Ms. Sophie celebrated everything she encountered. She stayed in the small saloon for five minutes. The room was only five hundred square feet and had a small bar and some lounge chairs and a small poker table. She was amazed with the floor-to-ceiling mirrors. She said that the mirrors made the room feel like it was twice the size.

I had never even noticed some of the observations that she made, and I had been on the boat hundreds of times. For instance, she asked me where the soft jazz music was coming from since she could see no speakers. I looked around, and I couldn't find any speakers either. I had never noticed that there were no speakers, not even in the walls or ceilings. Trying to appear that the boat was half mine, I pontificated that the speakers were ensconced within the walls. She bought it and was impressed.

I took Ms. Sophie belowdecks, where, in the stern, I showed Ms. Sophie the five cabins. Each cabin was paneled in a different kind of expensive wood. Since Ms. Sophie was the first guest, I said that she could pick her cabin. She chose the cabin with teakwood paneling. I then showed her one of the bathrooms. She was even impressed with the "luxurious" towels. They were fine, thick towels.

She then asked me where I slept. I took her to the servants' quarters, which had two bunk beds and was located toward the back of the boat, near the engine room.

She acted impressed with my quarters, saying, "You have this to yourself, and you even have your own bathroom."

When the tour took us by the walk-in wine cellar, you would have thought that she had just entered Disney World.

"Tommy, this is a beautiful wine cellar. What is the most expensive bottle of wine in here?"

"I don't know, Ms. Sophie. I'm not allowed to drink wine, so I don't concern myself with this room. Are you a big wine drinker?" I asked her.

"I love a good Pinot Noir, but it is usually poured out of a box, so I don't recognize any of these Châteaus,

Bordeauxes, and Rothschilds," she said in a fake snobby, elitist voice.

We both laughed. I was in love with this woman. She was something like nothing else.

By the time we finished the tour, four more people had arrived. Sophie took off running toward the crowd. Some of the new guests began running toward Sophie, and everyone was screaming and/or giggling. After the hugs and cackling died down, Sophie introduced me to Ben Eiler and Kelly White. Mr. Eiler and Ms. White acknowledged me but didn't take an interest in me like Sophie did. Instead they introduced Sophie to their spouses. I liked Lauren Eiler. She seemed very sweet, but I immediately hated Mr. Raymond White. I don't know why, but I could tell that he was a total dick.

The next to arrive was Steve Camp. He appeared to be a likeable sort. He came onto the boat with a Yeti cup, and I'm pretty sure that there was some vodka concoction in it. He gave hugs to everyone but held Ms. Sophie longer than everyone else. Ms. Sophie asked him where his wife was.

He said, "That's a story to be told after dinner."

Dr. Mason said, "Speaking of dinner, here's the plan. I am cooking steaks for everyone tonight. Each night, someone else is responsible for cooking dinner. The remaining two nights, we will have dinner at the two private clubs on Bald Head. One is the Bald Head Island Golf Club, and the other is the Shoals Club, which is a beach club located on the farthermost point of the island."

I didn't think I could like Ms. Sophie any more, but she surprised me when she excitedly said, "Golf? There's a golf course on the island? I would love to play a round if anyone is willing to go with me."

I wanted to raise my hand, but I didn't think Dr. Mason would like it since he was already expressing interest in the golf outing. The dick, Raymond White, announced that he was a 2 handicap and would love to play.

Steve Camp was the last to volunteer. "I am a 22 handicap, but I will play if Raymond doesn't mind playing with a weekend hack."

Sophie chuckled. Raymond blushed, and I determined that I liked Steve Camp.

Kelly White interjected, "Okay, we have dinner plans for the week, a golf game planned. How about we discuss lunch? I am starving."

Everyone looked at Dr. Mason

I could tell he loved being the center of the group's attention.

"So Freedom sent me a text saying that she would be late. Shocking, I know."

Everyone laughed.

Dr. Mason continued, "I suggest we head to the island's marina. There is a fantastic place in the marina called Jules's Salty Grub and Island Pub. They have great fresh seafood and an even better bar. After we eat, we will come back to Southport and meet Freedom."

Everyone agreed. That was my cue to set the sails.

CHAPTER 8

Dr. Theron Mason

I couldn't have asked for a better beginning to the week. Sophie looked even better than she did in college, and most importantly, she didn't have a plus-one with her. This week could change my life. I just needed to play it cool and look for my opportunity to tell Sophie how I felt. My other college friends were about what I expected.

Kelly seemed a little depressed. She had a put on a few pounds since college, but who am I to judge anyone for that? She was still very pretty. Her hair was still blond—no signs of gray. She has clearly invested in some plastic surgery, and she had ridded herself of those glasses that she wore in college. She looked good. I wonder why she seemed depressed. Maybe it was the fact that she hadn't had any children. Or maybe it was that her husband acted like we should all be grateful that he graced us with his presence on this trip.

Steve Camp was another interesting question mark. Where was his wife, and what did he mean when he told Sophie "That is a story that needs to be told after dinner"? He looked to be in great shape but also was drinking vodka at noon. He used to be the life of the party. Everybody loved him, and he made every moment better because of his presence. Today he barely spoke.

Ben Eiler married a sweetheart. Lauren had to feel a little awkward. She wasn't nearly as pretty as Kelly, and she couldn't hold a candle to Sophie. Yet she was a great conversationalist and seemed to have already befriended Sophie. I have always been jealous of people who are comfortable in their own skin and don't feel the need to compete with other people. Lauren was very content in being identified as the mother of eight children. She apparently didn't need anything other than her children to determine her self-worth. I sensed, though, that Ben was not as content with his life choices.

When we arrived at Jules's Salty Grub and Island Pub, we were told that we had a thirty-minute wait for a table. We didn't mind. They had a perfect outdoor bar area that overlooked the marina. Good conversations are organic. They can be intentionally initiated, but the life of the conversation will depend on factors that are totally unpredictable. We were all being friendly as we awkwardly asked each other about the day's travel adventures, but when a patron walked into the beach bar wearing a cowboy hat, the conversation took off.

"Hey, Steve, someone stole your cowboy hat," quipped Ben.

The five of us college friends began to laugh hysterically.

Lauren looked confused and said to Raymond, "I think we are missing out on an inside joke. Why are cowboy hats and Steve so funny?"

Since Ben made the joke, it was his story to tell.

"So in college, Steve had written up a bucket list. This was before bucket lists were a thing, but it was Steve's list of things he wanted to do before he died. One of the items on Steve's list was that he wanted to ride a bull."

With that, Lauren's eyes got big. She smiled and scooted her chair closer to the table. Raymond checked his phone for new emails.

Ben continued, "A small professional rodeo had hung posters around the campus, announcing that their rodeo was coming to the county fairgrounds in a few weeks. Steve had to be the only Furman student who even noticed the posters, but he came back to the apartment and announced that he was going to ride a bull in this rodeo."

Steve interjected, "How could I pass up such an opportunity?"

Everyone laughed, except Raymond.

Ben, sensing momentum, continued the story, "Steve called the producers and lied about his rodeo experience, claiming to be a professional bull rider from Jackson, Tennessee."

This statement interested Raymond; he set his phone down and began to listen.

"The rodeo producers agreed to add Steve to the list of contestants. For a couple of weeks, no one really thought about the rodeo, believing that Steve would chicken out as the date approached. However, the night before the rodeo, Steve came into the apartment with the DVD copy of the movie *8 Seconds*, a movie about Lane Frost, who was a famous and beloved bull rider who died tragically after being trampled by a bull at the conclusion of one of his rides. The night before the rodeo, Steve and I watched the movie, with Steve telling me to pause the movie so he could see how Lane Frost—played by Luke Perry—was holding the rope and how he wrapped his legs around the bull's torso."

Lauren put both her hands over her cheeks in astonishment. Steve held up his index finger as if to say "It gets better."

Ben continued, "Yes, yes, Steve was trying to learn how to ride a bull by watching a Hollywood movie. The one thing Steve did learn from the movie was that, after a ride, Lane Frost would always raise both his arms over his head and wave to the crowd with both hands. The next morning, we told everyone on campus about Steve's pending disaster. That night, half of the student body showed up to watch Steve."

Steve interjected, "I probably would have chickened out if the entire student body hadn't shown up to watch me."

Ben laughed and continued, "Steve went around the dorms asking to borrow a cowboy hat, boots, chaps, and everything else he would need. When we showed up to the rodeo, we could see Steve looking very much the part of a cowboy. We made eye contact with Steve, and he came over to the fence to chat with us. 'I'm fucked,' he said. 'We had to draw names for bull assignments, and I drew Hell's Fury. All the other cowboys groaned when I drew his name. They told me he was the biggest, meanest bull on the circuit.'

"When the public address announcer called Steve's name, the student body ceased their conversations and turned all their attention to the shoot where Steve sat atop Hell's Fury. The PA announcer was going on and on as he hyped up Steve. 'Yes, sir, we have *big, bad* Steve Camp hailing all the way from Jackson, Tennessee.' The announcer went on to read Steve's very impressive but fake rodeo resume. We were all wondering why it was taking so long to open the chute. Steve told us later that the reason for the delay was that they were teaching him where his hand should go on the rope and where his legs should straddle the bull's ribs.

"Finally the shoot opened, and this is exactly what the PA announcer said, 'Cowboy's in trouble! Cowboy's off!'"

Ben was trying to finish the story, but everyone was laughing so hard, including Ben that catching his breath was proving difficult.

After a few moments of laughter, Ben finished the story, "Hell's Fury had bucked one time, and Steve's face planted right into Hell's Fury's sternum, breaking Steve's nose and sending blood everywhere. Hell's Fury, sensing that Steve was losing the battle, made one quick turn, and Steve was sent straight into the ground. Understand, Steve didn't float through the air and land softly on the surface of the rodeo rink. No, it was like he had been shot out of a cannon, a cannon that was aimed directly at the ground."

The laughter subsided a little bit as people feigned concern for Steve's safety.

Ben concluded the story, "With his broken nose, blood dripping all over him, and his broken clavicle, Steve managed to raise both arms over his head and waved at the crowd as Lane Frost had done. The crowd booed him relentlessly and began throwing popcorn at Steve as he exited the arena."

Everyone laughed for several minutes—everyone except Raymond.

Lauren was still shocked about this story. She said, "Steve, I can't believe you did that. You were one crazy son of a gun."

Steve replied, "I was a bit crazy in college. I almost rode a bull while we were all in Mexico, but the rancher had just fed his bull and wouldn't let me ride him."

Everyone stopped what they were doing and glanced up at Steve.

Raymond looked at Kelly and said, "You all went to Mexico? You never told me that story."

CHAPTER 9

Kelly White

Since Bald Head doesn't allow any vehicles, each of us jumped into our rented golf carts to return to the boat. Raymond and I were alone for the first time since we arrived. I hated being alone with my husband. It didn't take him long to begin his inquisition.

"So, Kelly," he said with contempt, "why did you never tell me about this trip you and your college friends took to Mexico? That seems like a story that you would have told me while we honeymooned in *Mexico*."

"I don't know," I replied. "It wasn't that big of a deal. Actually we never intended to go to Mexico. We were supposed to go to Padre Island, on the southernmost point of the Texas coastline. Ben's uncle had a condo on Padre Island that we were going to stay at, but when we arrived, we discovered that we were going to be sharing the condo with Ben's aunt and uncle and their three kids. It wasn't exactly the spring break environment that we were looking for. On our second day, someone suggested that we go to Matamoros, Mexico—a border town just across the border from Brownsville, Texas—to shop and explore.

"While we were in Matamoros, Steve had the adventurous idea of spending our spring break by driving to

Mexico City. So we did. We drove to Mexico City, and we drove back. It just wasn't that memorable of a trip, so I never mentioned it to you."

"I don't believe you. There is another reason you never told me about this trip," Raymond said.

I sat in silence, not wanting to discuss it anymore. My marriage was so bad that I didn't care if he believed me or not. I certainly didn't trust him.

We sat in silence for the next few minutes.

As we approached the boat, Raymond said, "Why didn't you tell me that one of your friends is a felon?"

CHAPTER 10

Lauren Eiler

I liked all of Ben's college friends. Sophie was precious, and Steve was hilarious. I had hoped that Ben and I could take a beach vacation by ourselves, but this could be fun. I thought that Sophie, Kelly, and I might become girlfriends, which, with eight kids keeping me busy, were relationships that I was in desperate need of. In my old days, I would have been resentful of Sophie's and Kelly's beauty, but that was when my looks were something that I took pride in. That sense of pride no longer consumed me. Like any woman, I wanted to look my best, but I didn't have time to compete with the Sophies of the world, so why try? I am sure that Kelly and Sophie were somewhat jealous of me for having children. Great friendships can't be built unless both parties are a little jealous of their friend's life.

My thoughts were interrupted when Ben stopped the golf cart and directed my attention to the beautiful beach. There were dunes with beach grass blowing in the wind. It looked like the beach grass was dancing to the latest Iggy Azalea song (one benefit of being a parent to teenagers is being abreast of the latest hit music). The repetitive sounds of the waves lapping onto the beach provided the percussional beat to this song and dance.

"It's beautiful," I said to Ben.

Ben didn't respond. He looked deep in thought—like something was bothering him.

"What's wrong?" I asked him.

He didn't immediately respond but eventually said, "Look at those sand granules. That sand is eternal. No one can kill it. No one can stop it. It has been here since the beginning of time and will be here long after we are gone. Sure, it may get washed out to sea, but it comes back, or it may lie at rest somewhere else for decades. It may reside at a thousand different places, or it may lie at rest at one point forever, but that sand will never die."

I had no idea why Ben was contemplating the brevity of life, but something was going on. I touched Ben's hand, and he turned to me. Though he tried to hide it, tears were escaping his eyes.

He quickly refocused and said, "Come on. We've got to get to the boat to meet Freedom."

CHAPTER 11

Freedom Goforth

"Weston, can you get the bags?"

I took off down the dock. There they were—my old college friends. I couldn't believe that we were actually reuniting after sixteen years. I was running toward the group as they walked toward me. Then from the back of the pack, Sophie started running down the plank to meet me. How did she always do the little things to make you feel loved? We embraced and told each other how great the other one looked. Usually telling someone that they look great is just a platitude, but in Sophie's case, I meant it. She looked amazing.

Everyone else finally arrived. Hugs were given in abundance, and introductions were made. I introduced Weston as my significant other and expressed surprise that more people didn't bring a plus-one. Everyone was silent except for Raymond, Kelly's husband.

He said, "Well, I was told that we could bring our spouse or significant other...but not both."

He laughed. No one else thought it was funny. Kelly dropped her head in despair. Raymond ignored her dismay and continued to laugh as he took pride in his apparent joke.

"Let's get loaded up and head out to sail," said Theron. "I've got steaks to prepare, and we have plenty of wine for everyone."

Weston announced that he made a stellar vodka martini (which he did) and asked Theron if there was vermouth on the boat.

"I didn't get vermouth," replied Theron, "but there is a quaint grocery store on the island called Maritime Market. We will dock tomorrow, and you all can buy whatever food or wine you want. They have fresh meat and seafood and an extensive wine selection, but they don't sell liquor. In fact, there is not a liquor store on the island, which has always perplexed me. However, if you tell me what liquor you want, I will call Jack, who owns the Silver Peddler. He will go to the mainland and have liquor waiting for us at his store."

"The Silver Peddler?" Ben asked.

"Yeah," Theron explained. "The Silver Peddler was the name that island residents gave to a young girl who sold silver off the back of her boat in the Bald Head Island harbor back in the late '90s. She eventually opened a brick-and-mortar store on the island and kept the name that the residents had given her. After about twenty years, she sold the store to Jack, who has added some really cool home decor and beach art, but he retained the name."

Being narrowly focused on his martinis, Weston asked, "And he will get us liquor?"

"He will get you anything you want, assuming it's legal," said Theron.

CHAPTER 12

Sunday-Night Predinner Drinks

After I shortened the sails and anchored the boat, Dr. Mason asked me if I would mind being a bartender tonight.

"Mind? I would love it."

Dr. Mason smiled and said, "Let me rephrase that. Do you think your mom would mind if you tended bar?"

I told him, "My mom has me 'bartend' for her every night that she is at home. Plus she is so happy that I have an opportunity to meet smart and accomplished people. She won't mind at all."

I was trying to learn and understand Dr. Mason's inventory of wine and setting up the bar when my first patron arrived. Of course, it was Steve Camp.

"Tommy, my good man," he said. "How about a cabernet?"

"Coming right up," I said.

As I was pouring Mr. Camp's glass, Raymond White entered the room, asked for a glass of Pinot Noir, and took a seat next to Mr. Camp.

"Does your pretrial parole officer know that you are on a multimillion-dollar boat in international waters?"

Mr. Camp looked like his life just flashed before his eyes. "Excuse me," he sputtered to Mr. White.

Mr. White pulled out a badge of some sort and said that he knew that Mr. Camp was an indicted felon and was not allowed to leave the Southern District of New York without written permission from his parole officer.

"I can explain…"

But before Mr. Camp could offer an explanation, Ms. Freedom and her boyfriend, Weston, walked in. Ms. Freedom looked far better than she did when she had arrived at the dock. She was wearing a ball cap and leggings at the dock. Now she had let her long brown hair down and was wearing a short black cocktail dress. I must say, she cleaned up nice. She was probably five feet nine inches, and most of her height was in her legs. I noticed that she had a dolphin tattoo on her ankle, and suddenly I wanted to spend my life saving dolphins—or at least tell her that dolphins were my life's passion. Her boobs were bigger than Ms. Sophie's; they looked fake but perfect. My kudos to the cosmetic surgeon who created that masterpiece.

"Hey, guys, you all look nice," Ms. Freedom said to Mr. Camp and Mr. White.

Mr. Camp was still stunned by Mr. White's question and said nothing.

Mr. White got up from his chair, extended his arms toward Ms. Freedom, and said, "Freedom, the same thing can be said for you. Wow, you are stunning."

Weston put his arm around Ms. Freedom in a possessive manner as Freedom thanked Mr. White for the compliment.

Soon Ms. Kelly, Dr. Mason, and the Eilers joined us at the bar. Everyone was there except for the one person whom I was excited to see—Sophie.

Most everyone was drinking. The men were drinking red wine, and the women were drinking a sauvignon blanc that Dr. Mason had recommended.

The conversation was flowing more fluidly than even the wine. Everyone appeared to be having a great time—everyone except Steve Camp and Raymond White. Steve was still shaken by Mr. White's question, and Mr. White seemed to revel in the discomfort that he caused Mr. Camp. He wouldn't stop staring at Mr. Camp.

Finally Mr. Camp excused himself and left the bar. It appeared that he was headed toward his cabin.

CHAPTER 13

Sophie Simmons

"Well, Jed, I hate that she lost her volleyball match, but I am excited that you are one step closer to joining me on this amazing boat off the coast of a perfectly picturesque island."

Jed always said everything right. I hung up the phone feeling reinvigorated with the love that Jed and I shared. I was finishing my primping so I could join the others at the bar when there was a knock on my cabin door.

"Steve, I was just getting ready to come have drinks with everyone. Are you okay? You look pekid."

"Sophie, I am in so much trouble. I need to talk to someone, and you are the easiest person I know to talk to."

"Of course, come in," I told him.

Steve told me that he had been charged with insider trading and explained how he didn't think he had done anything wrong and certainly didn't intend to commit a crime. He told me that his wife had left him and he had not spoken to his children since the day that his indictment had come down. He started crying, and who could blame him? He went on to tell me that Raymond was a big wig with the Justice Department and had confronted him about being out of state without his parole officer's permission—though Steve had tried repeatedly to contact his parole officer to get permission.

I didn't know what to say to him, so I hugged him as he continued to weep.

"Steve, you are a good man. I don't care what anyone says. Nothing the FBI or the Department of Justice says will ever convince me that you are anything other than a great guy." I continued, "You are going through hell right now, but my heroes are those people who have been through hell and yet are still kind and loving toward others. That's *you*. I believe that this life will soon reward you for your determination and continued kindness to others."

His crying waned a bit, and he asked me what I thought our other friends would think.

"I don't know what they will think, but after what we did in Mexico, none of them should judge anyone."

CHAPTER 14

Dr. Theron Mason

"Theron, do you need any help cooking the steaks?"

It was Sophie checking on me. She was always so damn thoughtful. How did she know that I had been drowning in self-pity as I thought about my friends enjoying their drinks while leaving me outside to grill steaks?

She looked beautiful. You could tell that she had made a point to look her best. Her hair was wavy. It looked like Farrah Fawcett's hair from back in the day—except that Sophie's was black. She had put mascara on; her eyes were sultry and deep. She was wearing a dark-gray dress that hugged every inch of her body. The dress had a circle ring that held the dress together. The ring was placed between her breasts, exposing a significant amount of cleavage. Did she dress up for me? Did she expect me to express my love for her and want to look her best? Maybe she wasn't going to wait for me to make a move. Maybe she was going to tell me that she had wanted to be with me since college.

"Sophie, you are so kind. I don't need any help with the steaks, but I would enjoy your company. You were always my favorite friend...even back in college."

"Ah, that's kind of you to say," Sophie responded. "Look," Sophie said excitedly. "There are dolphins jumping near the boat." She pointed in the direction of the dolphins.

"Wow," I said. "In all my times on this boat, I have never seen dolphins before."

That wasn't true. I had seen hundreds of dolphins, but I was trying to make the night special.

"They look so happy," commented Sophie, "like they are in love with each other and don't have a care in the world."

I didn't know how to respond. Did she comment on the dolphins' love for each other as a segue into a conversation about our love for each other?

Stop it, Theron. You're being ridiculous, I thought to myself. *Or maybe I'm not.*

By now, I had overthought my response, and my thoughtful silence had ended the conversation.

We stood there watching the dolphins in silence. I wasn't very good at this communication thing—at least not communicating my feelings to the love of my life.

Finally I attempted to initiate a conversation that could lead to an opening that would allow me to express my feelings toward her.

"So I heard you got divorced." *My god, I'm such a fool. That sounded so harsh.* "I'm sorry, Sophie. That was rude. You don't have to talk about it," I said as I attempted to recover from my verbal blunder.

"No, it's fine," Sophie said. "He was a good man, but we had nothing in common. We're still friends, or at least 'friendly' toward each other. We are definitely both happier now that we are divorced."

"I'm glad that you are happy," I said. "I've always wanted nothing more than for you to be happy."

With that, I maintained my gaze with Sophie longer than comfort would dictate. To my great joy and relief, Sophie never broke our gaze. It was a moment—it was a powerful moment. She had feelings for me. Friends didn't stare into each other's eyes like that. My heart quickened as she walked toward me, handing me a glass of Opus Cabernet.

"To our future, may it be filled with love and happiness," I said as I lifted my glass toward her.

Sophie lifted her glass in response and said, "To love and happiness."

Our glasses clinked as we smiled and stared into each other's eyes.

This was my moment. I had acted the coward throughout all of college. In four years of college, I never gathered the courage to express my feelings toward Sophie. That was going to change tonight. I put my glass down and turned toward her. As the bulge in my pants brushed against her body, I put both of my hands gently on her face and leaned in.

"Theron, I'm sorry." She pulled away.

I was mortified. The bulge was instantly decimated as was my ego.

"I'm sorry I gave you the wrong impression. I have always thought that you were an amazing guy, but I have a boyfriend that I am in love with," she said.

I should have apologized for misreading the situation and salvaged a shred of my dignity. But I had waited twenty years to be with Sophie. To give up now was simply not possible.

"Sophie, why is it so impossible for you to envision us together? Nobody could take care of you like I will. I promise you that no one will ever love you as much as I love you. Hell, I named this boat after you."

"Wait, you named the boat after me? How? This boat is named *Nomism's*. How is that named after me?"

I shouldn't have told her that I named the boat after her. Now she saw me as either pathetic or as a crazed stalker. I was too far in, though.

"It's an anagram. Switch the letters of *Nomism's* around, and you get *Simmons*."

"Oh, Theron, I am so flattered. You should know that, since our freshman year, I have wanted to hear you say that you wanted to be with me. You were the one person in college whom I could see myself with. During my doomed marriage, my thoughts would often turn to you in my moments of solitude. I was quietly in love with you during college, and probably even after college. However, too much has happened since our freshman year. Mexico happened."

"Mexico?" I asked, surprised.

"Theron, I guess that I am the only one among us, but I still struggle every day with the guilt from what we did in Mexico. Being with you would be a daily reminder. I mean, the hands that you just placed gently on my face as you tried to kiss me are the same hands that killed that man."

I couldn't believe that she brought up Mexico, but to defend myself would only result in a fight.

So I ignored it and dejectedly asked her, "You were in love with me in college?"

"Yes, Theron. How could you not know? I always did special things for you. I would make cards for you on days that you had big tests. I mailed you packages with a letter and homemade cookies when we were away from each other during summer breaks. I would call you late at night, just hoping that you would invite me over. You never did. I did everything but get naked and ask you to take me."

"Well, getting naked would have worked," I joked. "I was a coward. I just couldn't believe that you would think of me like that."

"Well, I did. I'm still very fond of you, but a lot has happened since college. There's Mexico, and there is also the fact that I am in love with my boyfriend. I want to marry him, and I think he wants to marry me. You will always be the one that got away, but you did get away, and my heart has moved on. I'm so sorry."

CHAPTER 15

Sunday-Evening Dinner

I had just set anchor about one-half mile off Cape Fear Point. We were still close enough to Bald Head that we could hear the families enjoying themselves on the beaches on the eastern point of the island. The sun was supplying us with a prelude to what would certainly be a magnificent sunset.

My enjoyment of the promising sunset was interrupted by Dr. Mason. He was angry.

"Tommy, hurry your ass up. The steaks are almost ready, and I need your help in setting the table."

I had never seen the plates and silverware that Dr. Mason was using tonight. When Dr. Mason and I were alone, we ate from paper plates. Ms. Freedom and Mrs. Kelly were very impressed with the plates. Apparently the plates resembled Chihuly blown glass. I had never heard of Chihuly, but it must have been quite expensive.

Mrs. Kelly commented, "The colors are spectacular, sky blue, orange, a soft green, and subtle beige. It's like we are eating off a masterpiece."

Ms. Freedom replied, "We are. Each plate looks like an impressionist painting of the sun setting over the beach with its orange hue resting on top of the blue ocean with the beige sand and the green island fauna resting next to the ocean."

"Speaking of paintings," said Mr. Camp, "look at these oil paintings. This is a Claude Monet, and I'm pretty sure that one is a Cézanne."

"Do you think they are real?" asked Mr. Eiler.

"Look at this boat," replied his wife. "Why would you think he would buy this nice of a boat and then decorate it with reprints?"

"Good point," Mr. Eiler conceded as he nodded and looked around in amazement at the boat.

"I don't know much about art," said Mr. Walker, "but I know wood. That dining table must have cost at least twenty-five thousand dollars. The wood is solid mahogany, and the glass runner in the middle is at least eight inches thick."

"I bet the chandelier over the table cost about that much," said Ms. Freedom. "I looked at a much smaller but similar chandelier. The design is called a geometric pendant, and it diffuses the light perfectly."

"Well, either Theron has developed an exquisite taste after college, or he hired the most expensive interior decorator on the East Coast to decorate his boat," said Mr. Eiler.

Most of the college friends and their significant others had taken their seat at the table when Dr. Mason came down with the steaks. He and I began to distribute the steak and rice pilaf. The only friend who was not seated was

Sophie. She then appeared from the galley with a salad that she had prepared. Dr. Mason was clearly surprised that she had graciously prepared the salad and thanked her though he seemed irritated with her.

I noticed that Sophie had also prepared me a plate just outside the dining room. Her kindness was limitless. As I took my seat just outside the dining room, I was taken aback by just how quiet the dining room was. The only voices that I could hear were Mrs. Kelly talking to Mr. White. Mrs. Kelly was asking Mr. White about his job. Raymond White always spoke loudly, so I couldn't hear if any other conversations were taking place. All I could hear was Mr. White bragging about how important he was in Washington, DC.

"Prosecutors are the most powerful people in our government, and of all those powerful prosecutors, I am the second most powerful prosecutor in the nation. I decide who goes to prison and who does not. I decide who gets the death penalty and whom we let plead. I can ruin anyone's life and lose no sleep over it. So you better be nice to me."

I heard Mr. White laugh uproariously at his own "joke," but I heard no one else grant him even a courtesy chuckle. Mr. White was very arrogant; my momma would say that he was like a rooster who believed the sun rose just to hear him crow.

Finally I heard Mrs. Kelly suggest that Dr. Mason make a toast. Dr. Mason politely suggested that maybe Steve Camp should make the toast. Mr. Camp also declined. Finally Mr. Eiler stood up and saved everyone from the continued awkward silence.

"Raise your glasses," Mr. Eiler said. "To Theron, thank you for organizing this amazing reunion. May this week allow us to slip into the warm familiarity of our past friendships."

CHAPTER 16

Steve Camp

I had to admit—Ben's toast was well done. I didn't know he was such an orator. His toast made me long to reconnect in a meaningful way with my old college friends. I had a lot to tell them; but I didn't want these interlopers, particularly Raymond White, to be present for my confessional.

"I don't mean to be rude, but I would propose that, after dinner, just us old college friends gather on the deck for one drink, and then we will reconvene with Lauren, Weston, and Raymond for the rest of the evening."

"Of course," Lauren said. "You all take all the time you need. This is your reunion. I am just fortunate to be able to spend a week off the coast of Bald Head Island."

She was so sweet. Ben married well.

Weston said, "Leave the wine, and you can stay out there all night."

Raymond White said nothing but nodded in agreement.

On the deck of the boat, I finally relaxed. The sun was in its last stage of setting. There was a mystical orange haze that enveloped Bald Head Island. The boat swayed gently in the water, making you feel like you were seated in a thirty-million-dollar rocking chair. The best part of the evening, though, was escaping the glare of Raymond White.

I poured everyone a glass of wine from a few bottles of Caymus that I had commandeered from the galley. We sat in silence for a few moments, but the silence was not uncomfortable. Great friendships don't require you to acquiesce to the societal impulse to make shallow conversation. Though this group of friends had not seen each other for sixteen years, our interactions were the same as they were in college.

"Guys," I said, "you all have no idea how much I appreciate your friendships, and I am going to need to lean on those friendships for the next few years."

"What's going on?" Ben asked with as much compassion as he could muster.

"I was recently indicted for insider trading. It's a bullshit charge, but I face the real threat of spending a few years in federal prison. My wife left after the indictment, taking the boys with her. I haven't spoken with Cooper or Blake—the boys—since the indictment. My Wall Street friends don't want to associate with me. They worry that I am wearing a wire because they have all done exactly what I am accused of doing."

Freedom was the first one to speak. "Oh my god, Steve. I am so sorry. We are here for you. We will do whatever we can to get you through this ordeal."

Ben was next to offer support. "I am so sorry, my friend…and unlike your former coworkers, you are my friend. If you ever need someone to walk down the sidewalks of Manhattan with you or have dinner in the most public restaurant in the city, I would be honored to."

Theron was next. "For one week, we are on this amazing boat at one of the most beautiful islands in the world. Try to forget about what's happening in New York, and after this week, we will walk through this valley with you."

"Thank you, Theron," I said, "but it will be hard to forget. Raymond White confronted me and asked me if my pretrial parole officer knew that I was on a boat in international waters."

"Does he?" Theron asked.

I sheepishly responded, "I tried to call him for weeks to seek permission to make this trip. He never took my call and never responded to my messages."

Through tears in her eyes, Kelly spoke, "I am so sorry, Steve. Raymond is an asshole. I hate that I married the man, and I am sorry that I brought him on the trip."

"I'm sorry you brought him too," I said derisively.

"Why don't you divorce him?" asked Theron.

"Because he controls me financially. I never finished law school and haven't worked since I married him. All our money is due to a settlement that he got before we were married. He repeatedly tells me that I will get none of it if I divorce him. I'm trapped in this godforsaken marriage, and my only hope for escape is if Raymond dies."

Sophie and Freedom had moved next to Kelly and were holding her as Kelly sobbed into Sophie's shoulder. Poor Kelly. For the first time since my indictment, I felt sorrier for someone else than I did myself.

After a few minutes, Kelly managed to compose herself.

Sophie turned her attention back to my problems. "Steve, my boyfriend is a criminal defense lawyer. I don't know if he can help, but I know that, if he can, he will."

"Oh my god, you have a boyfriend?" Freedom asked. "Is it serious?"

"Yes," Sophie said as she tried not to smile amid mine and Kelly's misery. "He's the best thing that has ever happened to me. I am hopeful that he will be able to join us this week so you all can meet him."

Theron surprisingly walked away looking quite angry.

CHAPTER 17

Sophie Simmons

I really was going to do it. I had planned to tell my friends on the first night that I was going to tell Jed about Mexico, but with Steve's and Kelly's revelations, I didn't think it would be the right time. I was going to tell them, though, I promised myself.

Now that I was back in my cabin, I called Jed. I told him that I had volunteered his services in helping Steve. Jed laughed and said that he would be happy to help him for free. He explained to me how the feds always charged white-collar defendants with "wire fraud." According to Jed, wire fraud is a catch-all charge that they can indict anyone whom they don't like with. The problem is that it carries a twenty-year sentence, so defendants are pressured to cut a deal. As an example, Jed said that, if someone committed credit card fraud, they were subject to a two-year sentence. So the feds would add a charge of wire fraud to the indictment, and now the defendant was facing a twenty-year sentence for a crime that Congress prescribed a two-year maximum sentence.

That didn't seem fair at all. Now I was really worried about Steve.

"There's one more thing that I need to tell you," I said. "Theron expressed his love for me tonight. I told him that I was with you, that I loved you, and that I was very happy."

There was a long silence.

Then Jed said, "I'm driving to Southport tomorrow. Will Theron be willing to sail back to the Southport marina to pick your 'boyfriend' up?"

My voice was giddy. "Really? You're coming?"

"Absolutely, Sophie. I am not going to allow you to spend a week on a boat docked off the shores of a beautiful island with a man who owns the boat and is madly in love with you without me there as well. My jealousy won't allow it," he said while laughing with embarrassment.

"Jed, you have no reason to be jealous. He may be in love with me, but I am madly in love with you. However, if it takes jealousy to get you to join me this week, then I will make you as envious as the moon is of the stars."

As we often did when we were apart, we fell asleep with our phones still on so that it felt like we were together.

I wasn't asleep for long before I was awakened by loud voices and the jostling of furniture coming from Raymond and Kelly's cabin. He was screaming at her. I couldn't decipher what was being said, but I couldn't stay there listening to Raymond verbally abuse Kelly. I told Jed that he needed to get some sleep, so I was going to hang up and head up to the deck.

Despite the drama of the night, it was a beautiful evening. Most of the island was dark. While Old Baldy was no longer a functioning lighthouse, the Oak Island Lighthouse still worked and, like clockwork, would emanate its light into the sky. The moon was almost full, and the only noise was the water lapping up against the boat's hull.

My peaceful solitude was then interrupted by a staggering noise. Shit, it was Raymond, and he was clearly drunk. He stumbled my way, nearly falling overboard twice.

As he approached, he mumbled, "Sophie, what a pleasure to find you alone out here."

The way he said it sent chills down my spine. I told him that I was just heading back to bed and tried to move around him. He grabbed my waist and forced me to stay there on the deck.

"Don't go to bed yet. Keep me company for a while."

I debated my next move but decided to wait a few minutes to make my exit. In his condition, I did not want to anger him.

"I'll stay for a few minutes, but then I really must go to bed."

"Sophie, why couldn't I have married you instead of Kelly?" he asked.

Now he was the one who needed to be concerned about my anger.

"How dare you say that? Kelly is an amazing woman, and you are lucky to have her."

"She's fine, I guess, but I deserve a woman like you."

As he said that, his hand started moving up the back of my shirt as he stared at my breast.

"I'm leaving."

I started to try to wrestle away from his grasp. He grabbed me even tighter and pulled me so close to him that I could smell his vodka-drenched breath.

"Sophie, just give me one kiss. I promise, if you don't like it, I will leave you alone."

He was trying to kiss me. Hell, he was trying to rape me. I grabbed one of the empty wine bottles that Steve had left from our earlier conversation and smashed it over the top of his head. It startled Raymond long enough that I managed to wiggle free and run to my cabin, locking the door behind me.

I couldn't catch my breath. I was trembling and terrified. I expected him to break down my door at any moment. After hearing nothing, I realized that he was probably too drunk to pursue me. Conversely I realized that, had he not been drunk, I truly believe that he would have raped me.

I moved two heavy chairs in front of my cabin door and attempted to go back to sleep. Should I tell Kelly what her husband had done to me? Should I tell Jed?

CHAPTER 18

Weston Walker

Monday—

Last night was one of the worst nights I had ever endured. Since Freedom was hanging out with her friends on deck and Lauren Eiler went to bed early, I was left to entertain Raymond White. After hearing him brag at dinner about being the second most powerful prosecutor in the world, I didn't want to discuss too much of my business or personal life with him. Not that I had done anything illegal, but why poke the bear, especially when the bear had said that he got great pleasure out of destroying people's lives?

For most of the night, he seemed fine with that arrangement. My refusal to talk about myself allowed him the time to talk even more about himself. He regaled me with stories about taking down mobsters and drug cartels. To hear him talk, he was the bravest crime fighter the world had ever seen. In between his many drinks, he actually compared himself to a comic-book superhero.

Around 11:00 p.m., his braggadocious rantings finally came to a point.

"Weston, since you are a Hollywood film producer, you should make a movie about my life."

Say what? Who has the gall to suggest that a movie should be made about their life? I'd had the pleasure of meeting Muhammad Ali, President Barack Obama, and the Dalai Lama. None of them had ever hinted that a movie should be made about their life.

I wanted to tell the guy off, but since I would be on a boat with him for a whole week, I said, "Raymond, it sounds like your life would make a great movie plot. However, I only do romantic comedies. Your life story needs a producer who specializes in action or suspense movies."

Freedom would be proud of me. I handled his imprudence quite well—or so I thought until I heard his response.

"Weston, if I can make an exception in prosecuting you for tax evasion, I would think you could make an exception and produce an action movie about my life."

I was stunned and stared at him in silence.

"What?" he asked. "That seems fair, doesn't it?"

I was still unable to speak.

So he continued, "I promise you that my exception is far more valuable than your exception."

I was finally able to speak, but I felt like I needed to call my lawyer before I began. "What do you mean tax evasion?" I said. "You just met me. You don't know anything about me."

"Weston, I may have just met you, but with the apparatus of the entire United States government at my disposal, it doesn't take me long to learn about anyone that I meet."

All I could think was *What the fuck is happening here?* Sure, I had been creative in sheltering my taxable income, but I hadn't done anything that everyone else in my business hadn't done.

I was sipping on my scotch trying to imagine what my lawyer would advise me to do. After a few moments, we started to hear voices as the college friends were coming downstairs.

As Raymond got up to greet the group he said, "Think about it, Weston. We have all week to discuss things further."

As I sat on the deck, watching the sun come up, I was still shocked about Raymond's proposal last night. I had decided last night to not mention it to Freedom until after I had talked to my attorney. Unfortunately I was three hours ahead of my Los Angeles lawyer and had to wait a few hours.

My thoughts turned to how I could possibly finance a movie about Raymond White's life without bankrupting myself.

CHAPTER 19

Dr. Theron Mason

As I drank my morning coffee on the bow of the ship, my mind raced with regret. What a disaster last night was.

I couldn't believe that Sophie rejected me. I also couldn't believe that she was in love with me during college. I was so pathetic in college. I thought that I needed to become a rich doctor before any girl could find me attractive. It turned out that Sophie liked me more as a poor college student than she did since I became a successful doctor with a thirty-five-million-dollar yacht.

I don't know if we would still be together if I had acted while in college, but now all I was left with was conjecture. Until last night, I had hope. There was hope that I would be with Sophie, someone who had made every day since I met her mean something. Hope is a powerful thing, and to be without it is very painful. Until last night, the memories of her felt like home. Now I was left to imagine the remainder of my life without her. Actually I didn't have to imagine it. I was going to live it.

For the rest of the week, Sophie's presence would be nothing other than a reminder of my pain. I wish I could just send everyone home. I didn't want to be here anymore, and I certainly didn't want to meet Sophie's new boyfriend. Again, what an absolute disaster.

"Theron!"

Great, it was Sophie approaching me.

"Good morning," I said.

"Theron, I am so sorry about our conversation last night. I value your friendship so much, and I would be devastated if I lost you as a friend."

"It's fine," I said. "I shouldn't have shared my feelings with you, or maybe I should have shared them with you sixteen years ago. Regardless, it's not your fault. I don't want you to feel uncomfortable around me. If you cannot love me, then I want you to at least hold the memory of me with fondness. I'm sure I will be fine, eventually."

"Theron, you know I will always cherish you and our friendship," replied Sophie.

I thought that was going to be the worst part of the conversation, but alas, Sophie had more to ask of me.

"I know that it is wrong of me to ask you to do this, but Jed, my boyfriend, is going to be at the Southport marina at noon, and I was hoping we could sail back to port to pick him up. I know it's unfair of me to ask, but…"

"It's fine, Sophie. Lauren mentioned that she wanted to explore the island, and we need to get some groceries anyway."

"Thank you, Theron!" She gave me a hug and skipped away, clearly excited to see Jed.

Again, what a damnable disaster.

CHAPTER 20

Back to Bald Head

"Tommy, can you tell the guests that we will weigh anchor and hoist the sales at 11:00 a.m. to head to Southport and then we will go to the island to shop and explore all afternoon? We will leave the island around five," Dr. Mason said.

"Will do, Doc," I replied.

Mr. and Mrs. Eiler were swimming in the warm waters of the Atlantic Ocean when I told them about the day's plan. Ms. Lauren was visibly excited.

She asked me, "Tommy, when we get to the island, what would you suggest that we do?"

"Ms. Lauren, there are so many things to do. You have to visit the turtle conservancy, climb Old Baldy Lighthouse, and if it were up to me, I would kayak through the marsh."

"Thank you, Tommy. That sounds amazing."

I continued my quest to inform the guests of our plans. Mr. Raymond White was the next guest that I encountered. He had a large bandage on his head and looked like shit.

"Mr. White, are you okay?" I asked.

He didn't respond, just mumbled something. I told him about the day's plans, and again he mumbled.

I found Ms. Freedom and Mr. Walker on starboard side of the boat. Ms. Freedom was lying out in a bikini while Mr. Walker was pacing along the boat while on his phone. Ms. Freedom was lying on her stomach. Her bikini bottoms were one of those new cuts that could almost be considered a thong bikini. There was cloth around the waist, but it progressively tapered into a thong as it scaled down her ass. Her tan lines suggested that she didn't wear this bikini very often, which was probably why she was tanning her backside.

If Mr. Walker had not been pacing back and forth, I probably would have just stared at Ms. Freedom; but because I didn't want to be caught gawking at her, I decided to interrupt her.

"Ms. Freedom?"

She didn't respond.

I tapped her on her bare shoulder, startling her a bit. "I'm sorry," I said.

She laughed, took out her earbuds, and looked at me attentively. "I'm sorry, Tommy. I wasn't paying attention, and I don't know what's going on with Weston. He has been on his phone all morning."

After telling her of our plans to head to the island, she said that they were going to ride bikes, head to the beach, and do some paddleboarding. I wished them a good day and continued my assignment.

I was hoping to find Ms. Sophie in a bikini as well— no such luck. She was fully clothed at the very back of the boat. She looked to be having a very intimate conversation with Mrs. Kelly. They were both crying. I turned around with plans to come back, but Ms. Sophie heard me and looked to see who it was. She looked terrified when she turned around. I was happy to see a smile draw across her face when she saw that it was me.

"Oh, Tommy, it's you. I'm sorry," she said as she wiped tears from her face.

I quickly told them the plans, and Ms. Sophie thanked me. She told me that they would probably just go to the Maritime Market since it was her and her boyfriend's turn to cook dinner tonight. I suggested that, after they shop at the market, they go next door to Bald Head Blues for some very cool island wear.

She thanked me for the tip. Mrs. Kelly never looked up.

I never found Mr. Camp. I guessed that he was still in his cabin. Oh well, he would figure out that the plan had changed when I lifted anchor.

For a reunion of old college friends, there was a lot of tension on this boat.

CHAPTER 21

Sophie Simmons

This "vacation" was exhausting. First Theron announced his love for me, then Steve informed us that he was under indictment. Kelly was an emotional wreck because of her bastard of a husband, and then that same bastard tried to rape me. All that and I still had to inform my friends that I was going to tell Jed about Mexico.

Thank God, Jed was coming. I couldn't finish the week without him. Until he arrived, I was going to do everything in my power to avoid seeing Raymond.

I had decided to not tell anyone about Raymond's attempt to rape me.

I first thought about reporting him to the police, but it would be his word against mine. He was the deputy attorney general, and I was just Sophie Simmons. Besides, though I know that he would have raped me had I not hit him over the head with a wine bottle, I would have to admit to the police that he had only asked for a kiss and said that he would leave me alone if I didn't like it. Nope, going to the police wasn't a viable option.

I then considered telling Jed. I decided to tell him after we got off the boat. Jed would not be able to go a whole week without punching Raymond in the face if he knew what Raymond had done to me. Punching the deputy attorney general in the face is not a wise career move for a lawyer.

I struggled most with telling Kelly what her husband had done to me. I first thought that she deserved to know whom she was married to, but she did know. She may have not known the details of my encounter with Raymond, but she knew what a terrible man he was. To tell her would have only embarrassed her.

My plan was to never leave Jed's side and just get through this week. My plan was interrupted this morning when Kelly found me on the back of the boat. She sat down next to me and began to cry. Through her tears, she asked me what happened last night.

I replied by asking her what Raymond said happened last night.

"He came into our cabin drunk and angry, which is not unusual, but what was unusual was the blood that was pouring down his face. I sat up in bed and asked him what happened."

"What did he say?" I asked.

"He said, 'That bitch, Sophie, hit me over the head with a wine bottle.' I was shocked and asked why you would do that. You are the sweetest person I know."

I squeezed Kelly's hand and let her continue.

"He said, 'Hell if I know. She's fucking insane.' What really happened, Sophie?"

I wasn't planning on telling Kelly, but I also wasn't going to lie to her. I did skip the part of the conversation where he asked why he couldn't have married me instead of her. There was no reason to provide gratuitously painful detail. I told her that he had grabbed me and attempted to kiss me. When I tried to leave, he grabbed me even tighter, so I grabbed the wine bottle sitting next to me and struck him in the head. I then made my escape.

"Was he going to rape you?" she asked.

I was hoping that she wouldn't ask me that question, but I answered truthfully, "I felt then and still feel that, had I not hit him, he would have raped me."

My worst fears were validated. Kelly was apologetic but didn't seem surprised by her husband's behavior. I told her to stop apologizing; she had nothing to apologize for and nothing to be embarrassed about.

"You do need to divorce that man, Kelly. I know it will be tough financially, emotionally, and psychologically, but you must find the strength to leave him."

"I know," Kelly said. "I am not as strong as you Sophie. He will destroy me if I leave him. He will utterly and completely destroy me."

I hugged her. Kelly may have thought that I was strong, but I didn't feel strong in that moment. I was trembling like a leaf. I needed Jed.

CHAPTER 22

Steve Camp

I couldn't get out of bed this morning. Sure, a part of my paralysis was due to Raymond White's threats, but part of it was the pain I felt in seeing my old friends again. Not many people get to experience what it would be like to be dead. While I hadn't had any out-of-body experiences, I did catch a glimpse last night of what it would be like to be gone from the earth. I was trapped in this strange place where my old life was gone, my Wall Street career was gone, my wife had abandoned me, my kids wouldn't speak to me, and yet my old friends' lives were moving on.

Before dinner, I walked around the boat. There was Freedom giggling with her Hollywood producer boyfriend as she rubbed his leg with the side of her foot. I walked outside and saw Ben and Lauren on the phone checking in on their eight children. You could tell there was so much love in that family. I thought I could hang out with Theron, so I headed his way only to find him and Sophie having an intimate conversation while sharing a drink. My friends were great, but as I watched what life used to be like for me, I realized that I was not missed. My friends were kind, but they wouldn't miss me if I was gone. By gone, I meant prison, I tried to tell myself.

The boat was moving.

Come on, Steve. Pull yourself together.

Shakespeare said in *3 Henry VI*, "Let me embrace thee, sour adversity, for wise men say it is the wisest course."

I climbed out of bed, took a shower, got dressed, and headed out to embrace the sour adversity of my life.

My first encounter of the day was with Raymond. He acted like he was my best friend.

"Steve, good to see you awake."

I was going to ignore him, but I noticed that he had a bandage on his head.

"What happened to your head? I asked him.

"Not that I owe you an explanation, Steve, but I slipped on the stairs and hit my head."

"Okay," I said as I walked out of the room.

I saw Theron in the bridge. I wanted to check out the technology on this boat, so I headed in to visit with Theron.

"Hey, Steve, how ya doin' this morning?"

"Well, I've been better, but I'm good. Where are we going?"

Theron filled me in on the day's plans.

"So," I said, "now that Sophie will have her boyfriend here, that means you, me, and Tommy are the only single people on the boat."

Theron responded, "That would appear to be the case."

I asked him, "You want to join me on an epic quest to find a bar on the island?"

He laughed. "I already have reservations at the Wisp. It's a quaint bar overlooking the marina and Old Baldy. It also has some really good beers."

"Sounds perfect," I said.

CHAPTER 23

Jed Cummins

Where were they? I had driven six hours to see Sophie, and they were over an hour late. I knew their tardiness was not Sophie's fault. She was so excited when I told her that I was coming, I knew that she wouldn't be late. Besides, she was never late. Punctuality was very important to her. I usually wouldn't care about someone being late, but I was anxious to see Sophie again.

Sophie had changed my life. After my divorce, I had dated around and enjoyed the single life to its fullest. However, none of the girls that I dated held my attention. I had come to enjoy my single life enormously. I had a great group of lawyer friends and was content with being single for the rest of my life. Then I met Sophie. I wanted to marry her after our first date. After dating for a few months, I wanted to introduce her to my daughter. Sophie thought that I was moving too fast and told me that she wanted to take a break.

I'd dated girls and had had several serious girlfriends throughout my life. I'd been married, and yet no breakup or divorce ever got to me. I had never believed that we were born with one soul mate—someone that our happiness depended on being with. I could be happy with a lot of different women or no woman at all. I still don't necessarily believe in soulmates, but I can tell you that I can't be happy without Sophie. The month that she broke up with me was the hardest month of my life. I was physically ill the entire month. When I had a small fender bender with my daughter in the back seat, Sophie found out and reached out to me on Facebook to check on my daughter. After a month of silence, it was so good to hear from her. We stayed up talking on the phone the entire night. She met my daughter two weeks later, and we had been inseparable ever since. The last couple of days had been the longest I had gone without seeing her since we reunited, and it had been brutal.

Where the hell were they?

There she was. God, she was beautiful. She was on the bow of the boat waving at me.

Wow, that was quite a boat. Jeez, I had no idea that this Dr. Mason friend of hers had a multi-million-dollar boat. If I was dating anyone other than Sophie, I would feel jealous and maybe a little inadequate; but with Sophie, well, I had faith in me and Sophie.

"Hey, baby," I whispered as she jumped into my arms.

God, it felt good to hold her body again. I wish I didn't have to meet her friends. I was ready to take her. I was ready to take her right now.

I liked all her friends, but I don't think Dr. Mason liked me. Raymond White was excited to see the four handles of scotch and three cases of Heineken that Sophie told me I needed to bring. She was right; apparently beer and scotch were beneath Dr. Mason. He only drank wine though it was really good wine.

The boat ride to Bald Head Island was almost perfect. Sophie and I stood on the deck and caught up. It was great except something was bothering Sophie. I wanted to ask her about it, but I knew that she would tell me if something was up.

As we made our way around the island, I commented on the amazing homes that dotted the beachline of the island. Sophie informed me that, according to Theron, most of the houses on the island had names. She pointed out some of her favorites. There was the house named Big Fish, which had a pool in addition to its beachfront property. She pointed out Cape Watch Cottage, which had wraparound porches with a perfect view of the ocean. She also loved Shore Beats Work, which not only had a great name but also had a dune-free view of the beach. Because of the dunes, the views of the beach from most homes could only be seen from the second-floor balconies. This island was beautiful, and I was going to spend a week exploring this beautiful island with my beautiful girlfriend. Life was good.

CHAPTER 24

Ben Eiler

"Lauren, I am proud that you are my wife."

I didn't compliment my wife often enough, so she was taken aback.

"Thank you, Ben. Why did you say that?"

"Seeing how all of my friends adore you makes me remember why I fell in love with you. You really are an amazing person. I came here embarrassed of our life, but—"

Lauren interrupted, "You mean embarrassed of me."

"No, no," I insisted, but I was ashamed to admit that she was right.

I knew how beautiful Sophie was. Freedom and Kelly were quite attractive as well. Lauren was still pretty, but she couldn't compete with those three. What was so impressive was that she knew that they were considerably more attractive than her and yet she didn't let it bother her. She was confident, kind, inquisitive, and funny. She was still the girl that I had fallen in love with. I had forgotten Lauren, my wife, and only viewed her as Lauren the mom. I was a fool.

After assuring her that I was never embarrassed of her, I continued my soliloquy, "I was embarrassed because Theron is a very successful doctor. Steve is—or was—a successful Wall Street investment banker. Kelly married a very powerful DOJ official. Freedom is experiencing her dream and living with a successful Hollywood movie producer. Sophie is a social worker, but she may be the happiest of all of us. I am a midlevel manager in a corporate behemoth. I push paper and have pointless conference calls all day. What I have realized after watching you interact with my friends is that I am blessed. I have a great wife, and we are raising eight kids together. What more 'success' could you ask for in life?"

Lauren pointed left, telling me to take the next left turn in our golf cart. "Ben, Theron may be rich, but he does not seem happy. In fact, since the first night, he seems quite sad. Steve may have been a big-time investment banker, but you know the saying, 'The wind blows the hardest at the top.' Steve got so big that the government targeted him for unfair treatment. He doesn't get to speak to his wife or children. Can you imagine how sad you would be if you didn't get to speak to the kids? I sense that Kelly and Raymond's marriage is a charade. Kelly seems terrified of him. Freedom and Sophie seem happy, but neither one of them have children. I wouldn't trade places with them for anything if it meant that we didn't have our eight children."

I nodded as my eyes filled with tears.

Lauren continued, "We are the luckiest people on this boat. We shouldn't feel embarrassed. We should feel blessed."

Just then, we arrived at our destination. We rented a kayak and continued our conversation as we paddled around the inlet creeks of Bald Head Island.

The grass blowing in the breeze provided a picturesque backdrop as we watched egrets go about their daily activities. Osprey flew overhead, and the heron were so comfortable with our presence they almost climbed into the kayak with us. There was some fear as we watched alligators bask in the sunlight, or more accurately, the alligators watched us with a distrusting eye. It was a beautiful day spent with my beautiful wife. Lauren was right. I was blessed—certainly blessed—more than I deserved.

CHAPTER 25

Weston Walker

This island really was amazing. I wish I could enjoy it more. I had talked to my attorney, and he had given me four options. The four options were no different from the options that I had considered before talking to him. I asked him which option he recommended me to pursue. He told me that only I could answer that question. It was a phone call that cost me three hundred dollars and provided me with very little usable information. The only worthwhile advice that he gave me was to tell Freedom about my conversation with Raymond White. He suggested that Freedom should know of Raymond's threats to me so she could avoid talking to him about my work or my finances.

We were standing on paddleboards, slowly navigating our way around Cape Fear.

"Weston, what is wrong?" Freedom asked. She continued, "We are finally alone on this amazing island, and you haven't said a word to me."

"I'm sorry, Freedom. I do have something that I need to talk to you about."

After telling Freedom about everything that Raymond had said to me, she sat down on her paddleboard. I joined her by sitting down on my paddleboard. There we sat, floating aimlessly on our paddleboards. Neither one of us said a word for five minutes.

Finally Freedom asked, "Have you done anything illegal?"

I responded, "I don't think so, but my lawyer told me that there are over four hundred thousand criminal violations in our federal system. It's impossible for anyone to know, much less adhere to, every law or regulation."

I went on to tell Freedom about a book that my lawyer had mentioned. It's called *Three Felonies a Day*. The basic premise is that every white-collar worker commits, on average, three felonies a day without even realizing it. My lawyer also said that, because of the hundreds of thousands of statutes and regulations and the infinite number of interpretations of those statutes and regulations, a federal prosecutor could prosecute anyone they want to—regardless of how conscientious that person may have lived their life.

I repeated some of the examples that my lawyer had given me. "It's a federal crime to clog a toilet in a national forest. It's a federal crime to take a cat white water rafting in the Grand Canyon, and there are over four hundred thousand other crimes that we as citizens know nothing about."

Maybe I shouldn't have told Freedom everything my lawyer told me. She looked terrified, the same look that I was sure I had been wearing since last night.

Freedom said, "Wow, I guess that helps me understand how a great guy like Steve could be indicted."

We sat there on our board in silence for another five minutes.

Freedom finally asked me the same question that I had been asking myself since last night, "So what do we do about Raymond?"

CHAPTER 26

Sophie Simmons

It was my and Jed's turn to cook dinner for everyone. Kelly had spent the day with us as we shopped at the market and then shopped for souvenirs for Jed's daughter. I had asked Kelly to not mention Raymond's assault of me, and she managed to honor my request though Jed could certainly tell that something was bothering Kelly. I tried to be as normal as possible in front of Jed. I even managed to sneak into Bald Head Blues and purchase a cool golf shirt with a Bald Head logo on the lapel for Jed.

Jed had purchased a bunch of steaks, halibut, salmon, asparagus, shrimp risotto, and a basket of rosemary bread with olive oil to dip the bread in. He was excited to prove that he was worthy of the title grill master. By the time we all returned to the boat and sailed to our point of anchor for the night, it was already dark. Jed immediately headed to the deck to heat the grill. Kelly and I got a glass of wine and headed to the galley to prepare a menu of bruschetta as the appetizer, a fresh salad, and orzo with wilted spinach and pine nuts.

Kelly was so desperate to avoid her husband that she wouldn't leave my side all day. I don't know what it is about sadness, but it seems to make the heart look for a reason to laugh. I didn't know what I said, but Kelly began to laugh uncontrollably to the point that she had tears streaming down her face. Seeing her laugh instinctively made me laugh. Like all great laughs, it became contagious. Soon Steve, Freedom, and Ben had joined us. They asked us what was so funny.

In between my laughs, I managed to shake my head and say, "I don't know. I don't know."

That made them laugh. When I noticed that Theron had joined us and was laughing as well, I knew that this was a special moment.

When the laughing finally died down, everybody poured themselves a glass of wine and began helping us with dinner. I looked around and realized that there was no one other than us old college friends in the room. This was my chance.

"Guys, I have something that I need to talk to you about." I closed the door to the galley and began.

"I love Jed. We have discussed marriage, and I want to marry him. However, I am committed to having a marriage where there are no secrets between us. Nearly sixteen years ago, I made a promise to each of you that I would never talk to anyone about what happened in Mexico. I am here today to ask you to release me of that promise and let me tell Jed and *only* Jed."

"You've got to be kidding me!" said Theron.

Ben was next to chime in. "Sophie, I have been married to Lauren for a long time. We have a good marriage, and I have kept that secret from her. You can have a good marriage without telling Jed about Mexico."

"I never think about Mexico," said Freedom. "Why do you feel like you have to tell him? Just stop thinking about it like I have."

It was my turn to defend myself. "Guys, what we did in Mexico haunts me every second of every day. We reached through time to steal a life. He may have been a creep, but it was not for us to take his life. We stole decades from him. Time is the most valuable thing in this world, and we stole it from him."

Theron was visibly angry. "He was raping that girl, Sophie. What were we supposed to do?"

I responded, "We *think* he was raping that girl."

Theron was too angry to talk, so Steve picked up the argument. "Sophie, when that Mexican general invited us to stay with him, we all slept outside on his front porch because we were so creeped out by him, and with good reason. The next morning, we left as soon as we could because we were terrified of him. I wish to God that we hadn't forgotten our camera at his house, but we did. When we went back to his house to retrieve it, he was screaming at us to leave. I will never forget the hideous pair of holey red underwear that he was wearing when we walked into his house. That poor girl was in her bra and panties and was crying hysterically. Of course, he was raping her or was going to rape her."

"I know," I said. "I know, but did we really have to kill him?"

"Oh my god." Theron had now raised his voice. "Sophie, we didn't want to kill him. We were just trying to get that girl to go with us so she would be safe. He started fighting us. What were we supposed to do, leave the girl there to be raped?"

"Maybe," I said. "As bad as rape is, killing someone is even worse, isn't it?"

The guys were clearly angry at me.

Freedom stepped in to give them some time to calm down before they got even angrier at me. "Sophie, we didn't mean to kill him. When he started fighting us, Theron instinctively hit him with the fire poker. What else was he supposed to do? That psychopath would have killed all of us. We were witnesses to him raping a young girl."

Theron jumped in. "Wait a second. Don't blame me. I hit him on his back with that fire poker. That's not what killed him. It was you, Freedom, who hit him over the head with that vase."

After Freedom remained silent, Steve jumped in to defend her. "We all hit him with something. Who knows which blow killed him? I just know that it was a justified killing."

I agreed with Steve. "I think it was mostly justified, which is why I wanted to call the police immediately after we realized that he was dead."

Theron got in my face. "Sophie, stop being so damn naive. We were in Mexico. Our parents thought we were still at Padre Island. We didn't have cell phones back then. Nobody knew where we were. We had just killed a Mexican general. The young girl had run out the door during our fight with the psychopath. She couldn't verify our story because she had disappeared. No one would have believed us. We would still be rotting in a Mexican prison if we had followed your advice and called the police."

"Okay," I said, "I don't want to debate that decision again. I just want to tell Jed. Jed is a criminal defense lawyer. I will hire him first to be my lawyer and then tell him. Attorney-client privilege will attach, and he will be forbidden from telling anyone. He is the most understanding man I have ever met. I promise you all that you have nothing to worry about."

"Nothing to worry about?" Steve said. "I am facing felony charges. Imagine if my prosecutors or, even worse, Kelly's husband knew that I was an accomplice to murdering a Mexican general. I would never see the outside of a prison cell for the rest of my life."

"Sophie, I know you don't care about me," said Theron.

I interrupted, "That's not true, Theron."

He ignored me and continued, "I have spent my entire life sacrificing so I could have a successful medical practice. My medical license would be revoked if they even heard a rumor about me being involved in killing someone. Please, Sophie, please don't do this."

I didn't respond.

Kelly finally spoke in a very quiet voice. You could tell that she was choking back tears. "Sophie, I love you. You are the kindest person that I know. I know your heart is in the right place, but I am begging you to not tell anyone, even Jed."

Again I didn't respond.

So Kelly continued, "I know that we are asking you to carry this burden, but I am begging you to be strong and carry the burden. I have no idea what Raymond would do to me if he knew that I was involved in this, but I know that I would never experience another day of happiness for the remainder of my life."

I still didn't respond. Everyone was looking at me.

Finally I said, "Okay, I won't tell him."

My heart sank. I hated this secret. I hated that I would have a secret between me and Jed. I honestly didn't know if I could even marry Jed if I didn't share my secret with him. I know myself. This secret would slowly but surely destroy me and our marriage.

I hadn't noticed, but Freedom and Kelly were embracing me. Steve, Ben, and Theron had wrapped themselves around us girls. We were all hugging and were all crying—none so much as me.

CHAPTER 27

Monday-Night Dinner

I had spent the early evening helping Mr. Cummins cook the steak, halibut, and salmon. Mr. Cummins was cool. He kind of reminded me of Dwayne Johnson. He was strong—for an old guy. He was bald, but he had shaved his head. It looked good on him.

"Mr. Cummins, have you been to the Old Baldy Lighthouse yet?"

"No, Tommy, I haven't yet. Is it cool?"

"Oh, Mr. Cummins, it is so cool. You have to go. After all, it's called Old Baldy, and you are old and bald."

I thought my joke was funny, but not as much as Mr. Cummins did.

He laughed harder than I did and told me, "That was a good one, my young friend. You got me."

I was relieved that he found humor in my joke and knew that I liked this guy.

He was very curious about my life. I could see why he and Sophie got along so well. He also poured me some of his scotch—on the condition that I tell no one else.

"Tommy, thank you for your help and your company. Why don't you go tell Sophie that the meat is about ready?" Mr. Cummins asked.

"Yes, sir," I responded.

I was happy anytime I had a reason to talk to Ms. Sophie. I found Ms. Sophie and her college friends all coming out of the galley together. I was confused. They looked like they had been crying, but they seemed happier than they had appeared all week. Even Dr. Mason seemed like he was in a good mood.

"Ms. Sophie, your boyfriend wanted me to tell you that the meat is almost done."

"Thank you, Tommy. We are headed upstairs right now with appetizers."

I followed them from behind, fixated on Ms. Sophie's legs as she climbed the steps to the deck. As we approached the deck, I noticed Mr. White and Mr. Cummins were talking. Mr. Cummins was laughing. For the first time this week, Mr. White seemed to have found a friend.

Mr. Walker was sitting on the other side of the deck talking to Mrs. Lauren. The group of college friends walked past Mr. Cummins and Mr. White and sat down next to Mr. Walker and Mrs. Lauren.

Dinner went without incident. Everyone was enjoying the wine and complimenting Ms. Sophie and Mr. Cummins on the meal. Mr. White and Mr. Cummins sat next to each other and continued their conversation. Everyone else ignored them and seemed to appreciate the fact that Mr. Cummins was occupying Mr. White's attention, thereby letting them enjoy an evening without his braggadocious interruptions.

Everyone seemed happy, and thanks in large part to Mr. Cummins's scotch, this was developing into my best evening of the trip. There seemed to be less stress. The sun was setting over the island, and there was a very pleasant ocean breeze blowing across the deck. Nights like this made me want to study hard, get good grades, and become rich like Dr. Mason so I could afford a boat like this.

Mr. White suddenly stood up and announced that he had some work to do, so he was going to head to his cabin early. No one seemed disappointed to see him leave.

After Mr. White left, Dr. Mason asked me to go prepare the mainmast for the night and to drop the second anchor. I headed off a little lightheaded from the scotch but still managed to complete my task rather quickly. I then snuck back to the promenade deck, where I could hear the friends' conversation on the quarterdeck. I was glad I did—what a conversation it was.

It began with Mr. Cummins asking Mr. Camp about his indictment. It seemed crazy to me that Mr. Camp was in trouble with the law. He was so nice.

"Well, Jed, it's not going great," said Mr. Camp. "Raymond confronted me on this trip asking me if my pretrial probation officer knew that I had left state lines and had ventured into international waters."

"I take it that your parole officer doesn't know?" Mr. Cummins asked.

"No, I tried to tell him, but he would never answer his phone, and he never called me back," Mr. Camp said.

"Why would Raymond White care about whether you had violated the conditions of your parole?" asked Mr. Cummins.

Mr. Camp responded, "He told me that I needed to give him—and him alone—information that would lead to the indictment of the CEO of my company or he would notify my judge and seek to have my parole revoked."

Mr. Cummins responded, "Unfortunately that's how many prosecutors work these days. Y'all are being too harsh on him."

Ms. Freedom objected, "Jed, I'm sorry, but you are wrong about Raymond. Weston, tell them what Raymond said to you last night."

Mr. Walker was silent for a bit but eventually began telling his story. "Last night, while you all were talking, Raymond began regaling me with stories about his crime-fighting heroics. He then asked me to produce a movie about his life. I was shocked at his narcissism and told him that I didn't make movies like that. He then threatened to prosecute me for tax evasion if I refused to make his movie. I don't think I have done anything wrong, but my lawyer says that, if the government wants to indict you, they can find a crime in anyone's financial past. I am scared to death. There is no way that I can sell a movie about Raymond White to any investors, which means that I will have to empty my savings to make his absurd movie."

"Damn," said Mr. Cummins, "that's unbelievable."

"Was he drunk?" asked Mr. Eiler.

"Yeah, he was definitely drunk," replied Mr. Walker.

Mr. Cummins followed up with another question, "Has he said anything to you today about his movie?"

"No," Mr. Walker said, "but I've done my best to avoid talking to him today."

Mr. Cummins again tried to give Mr. White the benefit of the doubt. "Well, maybe he was drunk and doesn't even remember the conversation."

"I hope you're right, but I have my doubts," said Mr. Walker.

CHAPTER 28

Sophie Simmons

Tuesday—

Last night was tough. Listening to Jed defend Raymond made my stomach turn though the fact that Jed always saw the best in someone was one of the reasons that I loved him so. This morning reminded me of another reason why I loved him. I awoke with a cup of coffee sitting on my nightstand and Jed rubbing my back. As much as I loved it when Jed rubbed my back, I knew what it was going to lead to. This morning, I didn't mind. In fact, I wanted to feel him inside of me. I had never loved morning sex, but Jed had a way to drive me crazy—even in the morning.

As much as I enjoyed our much-needed morning "session," it put me behind schedule. We had a tee time scheduled for 10:30 a.m. I wasn't going to go golfing, but Raymond announced that he was unable to play due to his work requirements and his need to prepare for dinner since tonight was his and Kelly's turn to make dinner for everyone. Honestly I think he backed out of golf because he didn't want his claims of being a scratch golfer to be discovered as fraudulent. Regardless, I was thrilled to spend a day without worrying about encountering Raymond.

Theron also backed out of playing. He didn't give a reason, but I suspect that he didn't want to spend the day watching Jed and me enjoy each other's company. I couldn't blame him. He was still kind enough to sail us to the marina so that Jed, Ben, Lauren, and I could play a round (Lauren wasn't golfing; but she was excited to ride around on the golf cart, enjoy the company, and take pictures of the scenery).

Bald Head Island Club was the most beautiful course that I had ever played. The course designer did a spectacular job of creating a golf course without altering the North Carolina coastal landscape. There are no cart paths because the sod is so perfect, and the course drains so well that concrete paths are not needed. The course snakes its way through the island's maritime forest, lagoons, massive live oaks, and natural dune ridges. It did take some adjusting to hit a long iron while alligators glare at you with their hungry eyes. The tee box on the sixteenth hole is the highest point on the island. You can see almost the entire island and a panoramic view of the Atlantic Ocean.

Jed took me golfing for the first time about a year ago, and I fell in love with the sport immediately. I had improved dramatically since my first attempt but still had a long way to go. I didn't care, though. I loved golf because it reminded me of my love for Jed. Most holes begin with a driver—an explosive shot that you hope travels a great distance. Similarly my and Jed's relationship began with an explosion of romance and intensity. Like a drive that eventually had to come down, I knew that the excitement of new love would not last forever, but I wanted to extend it for as long as possible. The next shot that follows the drive usually requires a fairway iron. The shot is less intense; instead it requires finesse and a constant attention to feel and detail. Our relationship was currently in that stage. Our love may not have been as intense as it was in the beginning, but it was more real. It was nurtured by constant attention to one another's feelings. It required finesse as we navigated the fact that he was a father first and foremost.

Like many golf shots that are misguided, love can be misguided. You can begin with an amazing drive or exciting first love, but you are unable to maintain those good shots or real love. However, when you can combine the excitement of a great drive and meticulous approach shot with a subtle but perfect putt, you have accomplished something beautiful—much like finding a lasting love.

I loved the way that Jed and I interacted with Ben and Lauren. For the first time, Jed and I had "couple friends." During Jed's divorce, he lost his old couple friends and surrounded himself with work friends and old college-football friends. Because my ex-husband was so busy with work, we never had couple friends either. I could tell Jed was enjoying himself as he traded insults with Ben. I had never understood why men find so much humor in insulting each other, but as long as Jed and Ben were having fun, Kelly and I were content to have our own more emotionally significant conversations.

A couple of weeks ago, Jed took Luke, a lawyer friend of his, on a golf outing. Luke's wife had recently been diagnosed with a very aggressive form of cancer. The couple had three children under the age of twelve, and Jed thought it would be a nice distraction for Luke to take him out for a day of golf. That same day, I went to the hairdresser. That evening, over dinner, I asked Jed how Luke was handling his wife's cancer.

Jed responded, "I guess he's doing okay."

I asked him if Luke and his wife had told their children of the cancer.

Jed said, "I don't know. I didn't ask him."

I was surprised and asked Jed, "You spent five hours with a friend whose wife is dying from cancer, and you know nothing about how they are handling it? What did you all talk about?"

Jed said, "I don't know. We talked a lot about whether we could get the golf cart up to a speed that would allow us to catch air as we ramped this hill. We did manage to get some air on the attempted jump. It was awesome."

"Jed, you didn't talk once about the fact that his wife is dying? You didn't talk once about her cancer? I spent one hour with my hairdresser, whom I first met today, and I know everything about her, including what her husband's cum tastes like. I will never understand men."

Jed laughed and said, "You don't have to understand me as long as you love me."

I did indeed love him.

CHAPTER 29

Jed Cummins

Since I didn't bring my clubs with me, I had to rent a set of clubs from the golf shop. They were a nice set of clubs, but since they weren't mine, I had a ready excuse for my poor play. I was a 12 handicap. Sophie didn't have a handicap yet, but she got better each time she played. I was jealous of her constant improvement. I had played golf off and on since college. Since Sophie took up the game, we played twice a week, which was more than I had ever played. You'd think that my game would improve with that much practice, and yet it was as sporadic as ever. Some days, I played well enough that I fostered illusions of practicing hard and joining the Senior Professional Golf Tour after I retired. Other days, I wanted to throw my clubs into a pond and give the game up forever. Today was a good day on the golf course.

Bald Head Island Club was a beautiful course. It was designed by George Cobb, famous for his design of the par 3 course at Augusta National and over one hundred other Southeastern American course designs.

Ben was the perfect playing partner. We had comparable skills, so our match was competitive. He wanted to win but not to the point of sacrificing good conversation. We enjoyed laughing with and at each other.

I was also enjoying the round because I could spend hours watching Sophie in her little golf skirt. She was so damn beautiful. By watching swing lessons on YouTube, she had developed a perfectly elegant swing. The ball did not travel very far, but it was always straight as an arrow. On the third hole, she did something that only Sophie would do—she took off her golf shoes and played barefoot. She claimed that the reason she did this was because she could feel the undulations of the greens better, but I know her—she did it because she wanted to experience the golf course to its fullest, including feeling the perfectly mani-cured thick grass between her toes.

I enjoyed getting to know Ben. Good guy. He could take a joke well.

When I found out that he had eight kids, I said, "Eight kids? You do know that you can do it just for fun, right?"

Ben laughed and said, "Yeah, raisin' 'em ain't nearly as fun as makin' 'em."

I knew he could take some joshing, so I started calling him Bobby Kennedy. I was surprised that he was as good at golf as he was, considering he had eight kids vying for his time.

Ben and I were betting one dollar per hole. After Ben sliced his driver into a part of the course that the elk go to die, I won the twelfth hole. Ben paid me the dollar that I had won and then gave me an extra dollar and asked me if he could hire me as his attorney. He explained that he had a concern that he wanted to ask me about but wanted to be assured of my confidentiality.

I took his payment and asked him, "What's your concern?"

"Jed, Raymond made a comment to me that I didn't take very seriously until last night. When I heard what Raymond had threatened Weston and Steve with, I became concerned with the comment that Raymond made to me."

"What did Raymond say to you?" I asked.

"He asked me about my job with Coca-Cola. I hadn't told him that I worked for Coca-Cola and was a little taken aback by the question, but I figured that Kelly had told him where I worked."

"Makes sense," I replied.

Ben continued, "After telling him that I was a vice president at the company, he said, 'Looks like your efforts in Uganda paid off for you.'"

"Why would that comment concern you?" I asked.

"Well, first I'm not sure that Kelly even knew that I was in Uganda. How could Raymond know that I spent three years in Uganda? Secondly—and I need your confidentiality for this part—I directed a large portion of US Aid's Ugandan fund to Coca-Cola's international expansion into Africa. It was a legitimate use of economic development money, but I was negotiating a job with Coca-Cola during the same time that I was directing money to their expansion efforts. There was no explicit arrangement or quid pro quo, but in the eyes of an aggressive prosecutor, who knows?"

I took a few moments to digest everything that Ben had told me. I then said, "Ben, I don't think what you did was illegal, but regardless, the statute of limitations has long run on anything that happened in Uganda. I doubt Raymond knows anything about what happened in Uganda."

"I hope you are right because, regardless of whether or not the statute of limitations has run, I will lose my job if there is a hint of impropriety in how I obtained that job."

"I think you all are overreacting to Raymond." I continued, "He is certainly a prick, but I can't imagine him being as evil as you all have made him out to be. Kelly has a right to hate him, but I don't think he is the menace that you think he is."

On the fourteenth hole, I pulled my drive into the lagoon that ran the left side of the fourteenth fairway. After taking my drop, I feathered a nice 7 iron into one of the bunkers that surrounded the green, took two shots to get out of the bunker, and then three-putted for an eight. On our walk back to the carts, I quoted for Ben a poem that I heard somewhere.

> In my hand, I hold a ball
> Quite dimpled and rather small
> Oh, how bland does it appear
> This harmless-looking little sphere
> By its size, we'd never guess
> The awesome power it does possess
> For since we've fallen beneath its spell
> We've wandered through the depths of hell
> To master such a tiny ball
> Should not be very hard at all

But our desires the ball refuses
And does exactly as it fuckin' chooses
It hooks, it slices, it dribbles, it dies
It disappears right before our fuckin' eyes
Sometimes it will have whim
Hit a tree, take a goddang swim, why
don't you
With miles of grass with which to land
It finds a scrawny patch of sand
It has us offering up our soul
If only it would find the damn hole
It has us whimpering like a pup
We swear we are going to give the damn
thing up
But we take to drink to ease our sorrow
Because the ball knows we'll be back
tomorrow

CHAPTER 30

Kelly White

I woke up dreading today. I was grateful to discover that Raymond wasn't in our room when I awoke. I was supposed to spend all day with him. We were scheduled to go to the beach at Cape Fear and then head to the market to buy food for dinner tonight. I couldn't bring myself to spend one more day with him—not after what he had done to Sophie, Steve, and Weston. I woke up determined to tell him that I was going to the island by myself and, when we got back to DC, I would be filing for divorce.

The door to my cabin opened, and Raymond entered with a cup of coffee.

"Did you get me a cup of coffee?" I asked.

He curtly replied, "No, I did not."

"Raymond, I am not going to go with you today. If you want to go to the beach all day, you can. I will go to the market and cook dinner tonight, but I don't want to spend the day with you."

He looked furious but said nothing.

Since I was experiencing a rare moment of bravery, I decided to continue. "Also, when we get back to DC, I am going to file for divorce."

He started laughing. It was a villainous laugh, not the kind of villainous laugh that you would hear coming from a Hollywood villain. It was far more subdued, but at the same time, it was far more sinister than anything Hollywood could manufacture.

"Kelly," he said, "you are welcome to go to the island without me. In fact, I would prefer to spend the day without your annoying presence. Feel free to cook dinner. I'll make my acquaintance with a bottle of twenty-one-year-old scotch while you cook."

"I *am* going to divorce you," I said.

"Kelly, I know that you and your friends murdered General Roderigo Sanchez. You're not going to divorce me or question me again for the rest of your life."

I was so terrified that I could barely catch my breath. "Who is General Roderigo Sanchez?" I asked with a trembling voice.

"Oh, you don't remember the name of the general that you and your friends murdered? Well, after overhearing your conversation last night, I did some research and read about the mysterious death of General Sanchez. The Mexican government spent millions investigating his death and even asked the United States to assist them in identifying the culprits. They theorized that he was murdered by foreign terrorists or a drug cartel. Turns out he was murdered by some American college friends." With that statement, Raymond resumed his diabolical laugh.

"What are you going to do with this information?" I asked.

"Well, I have been considering that question all night. I figure I have two options. First I could share what I know with the Mexican government and be an international hero for solving a sixteen-year-old mystery. General Sanchez is the highest-ranked Mexican official to ever be murdered without bringing the culprit to justice. If I turned my own wife and her friends in, I would be a media hero. By turning in my wife, I would be lionized for my adherence to the rule of law. I suspect that I would be the next attorney general of the United States. Not a bad option. My second option is to *own* you and your friends."

CHAPTER 31

Dr. Theron Mason

What to do today? I had declined to play golf today. I just couldn't spend a day watching Jed and Sophie flirt with each other all day. I was looking for Steve on the deck to see if he wanted to head back to our bar and drink our sorrows away when I ran into Kelly. She was crying.

I hugged her and asked her, "What's wrong?"

"Theron, if you will go onto the island with me and pick up food for tonight, I will tell you all about it."

"Of course," I said. "You don't need to bribe me with the disclosure of what's bothering you to entice me to spend the day with you. I would love to hang out with you."

She looked up from our hug and smiled. Once we got onto the island and into our golf cart, she began to tell me about the threats that Raymond made this morning. She told me that he had overheard us talking about Mexico and knew everything, including the name of the general whom we had killed. She told me that he was going to either turn us in or extort us for everything we had for the rest of our lives.

"Do you really think he would turn us in if it meant that his wife would spend the rest of her life in prison?" I asked her.

"Oh, Theron, you have no idea. He would relish the opportunity to turn me in."

"Wow," I said. "Kelly, you deserve so much better than him. I hate that you are in this position."

"Theron, forget about me. How about you? How about your medical license? How about your reputation, your future?"

She was right. I couldn't believe that I had not thought about how Raymond's extortion would affect me. Why, in that moment, did I only care about Kelly? Oh, shit, not again. Was I developing feelings for Kelly?

We spent the entire day together. By lunchtime, we had put a pin in the discussion about Raymond. Instead I took her on a tour of the island. I showed her the island's maritime forest and Old Baldy Lighthouse. We were having a great time together, even laughing occasionally. Then we passed the island's chapel. Kelly asked me to pull the golf cart into the chapel's parking lot. She grabbed my hand and escorted me into the chapel, where she led us in prayer. We asked for forgiveness for Mexico and prayed for wisdom as we dealt with Raymond. I couldn't say the chapel was fun, but it was a special moment that I shared with Kelly.

It was getting late, so we headed to the market to shop for dinner. Kelly never asked me to help her with preparing dinner. But I knew Raymond wouldn't lift a finger to help her, so I assumed responsibility. Since we had enjoyed steak and fish the two previous nights, I suggested that we prepare an Italian feast.

We bought ingredients to prepare Bellinis for a predinner drink, pizzette with prawns for an appetizer, an Italian salad with crispy breadsticks, and a spicy caponata as the entrée. I also selected a few bottles of my favorite Chianti to serve with dinner. We then went back to the boat and prepared dinner together. On the day that I learned that the deputy attorney general was determined to destroy my life and the lives of my friends, I managed to have the most enjoyable day I'd had in a very long time. Go figure.

CHAPTER 32

Tuesday-Night Dinner

Something was different about tonight. Mr. White had spent all day in the main cabin drinking scotch. Everyone else was upstairs on the deck talking in hushed voices. Tonight was the Whites' night to prepare dinner for everyone, and yet the grill had not been touched. I didn't know what everyone was whispering about, but I was hungry. Dr. Mason noticed me standing around and came over to talk to me.

"Tommy, there is some real shit going on tonight. Ms. Kelly and I prepared an Italian dinner earlier. It's in the Viking fridge. Would you mind turning the ovens to about 350 and warming up all the dishes? Obviously leave the salad in the Viking."

"Will do, boss," I replied.

As I walked to the galley to prepare my gourmet feast, I passed Mr. White.

He asked, "Tommy, what's going on with dinner? I'm starving."

"Well, Mr. White, I am going right now to warm up some food."

"Why are you warming up food? Why isn't my wife cooking dinner?"

"On account of them talking about something. They have been circled up whispering for over an hour."

Mr. White began to laugh. "I bet they have been talking. I bet they have. They have a big decision to make by the time we leave this boat."

I was very curious as to what he was talking about, but I didn't think it was my business. I didn't want to have to talk to Mr. White any more than I had to. He creeped me out. I said okay and made my way to the galley to prepare dinner.

CHAPTER 33

Chief Walter Denton

Wednesday—

I'd been offered more glamorous jobs on the mainland, but I'd turned them all down. The primary reason I turned those jobs down was because of how much I enjoyed my mornings on the island. This Wednesday morning, like every morning, I was sitting on my back deck with a cup of coffee as I gazed at the dunes and listened to the waves gently crashing in. I could hear children playing and family dogs barking on the beach though I couldn't see them because the dunes blocked my view (which I counted as a bonus). Gulls and fish crows cawed as they scoured the ocean's surface looking for their next meal. I enjoyed watching the sandburs, beach stars, yuccas, and Spanish bayonets dance in the morning breeze. It was a time of peace and solitude that could never be replicated on the mainland.

Unfortunately it was the last time for a long time that I would have any peace. My phone rang; and my only officer, Kevin Stitt, was in a panic.

"Chief Denton, I don't know what to do. I don't know what to do."

"Slow down," I said. "Take a deep breath and tell me exactly what's going on."

After a long exhale, he said, "Chief, there's been a body wash ashore on the Cape Fear beach. He was discovered this morning by some honeymooners who were on a morning jog along the beach. I have no idea what to do. The biggest case I have handled was a stolen bicycle. I need your help."

"Okay, I'm on my way. Don't touch anything and keep people away from the body. Move them far enough away that they can't take pics or videos with their phones."

Officer Stitt wasn't the only one who had no idea what to do. Bald Head is not only a sanctuary for wildlife and fauna but also a sanctuary protecting its residents and guests from the crime that afflicts so many other communities. In the latest crime statistics, Bald Head Island had only twenty-four crimes committed in the entire year. Of those twenty-four crimes, zero were violent crimes. Theft of bicycles was the number one crime reported on the island.

The last notable crime on Bald Head Island was well before my time. In 1999, Davina Buff Jones was one of the few Bald Head Island police officers on the island. On one stormy night, her body was found not far from the Old Baldy Lighthouse. Since the Bald Head Island police office was not equipped to handle a possible murder investigation, certainly not one whose victim was one of their own officers, they asked the North Carolina State Bureau of Investigation and then district attorney Rex Gore to investigate the suspicious death.

District Attorney Rex Gore ruled Jones's death as suicide. She had been under treatment for depression, and she'd recently broken up with a boyfriend.

Jones's family was unconvinced. For one thing, Jones was shot in the back of the head at an angle that would be virtually impossible for even the most determined suicide to try. She was taking her antidepressants, and her papers and effects indicated she was planning for the future, not contemplating a final exit.

Then there were her final calls to the Bald Head Island dispatcher, indicating she was "down with three," police lingo indicating she was leaving her vehicle to confront three possibly suspicious unknown individuals. The dispatch recording then picked her up saying, "There ain't no reason to have a gun here on Bald Head Island, okay? You wanna put down the gun."

Investigation of Jones's death scene would not have passed *CSI* standards. The body's hands, for instance, were not bagged to preserve possible evidence under her fingernails. As of now, Jones's cause of death is listed as undetermined, and barring a jailhouse confession, it's unlikely this cold case will ever warm up.

I didn't know if the body that had washed up on shore was a murder or just a drowning, but I didn't want to screw this case up as my predecessors had done with the Davina Buff Jones case in 1999.

My bungalow was only a few streets down from the Cape Fear beach, so even in my police golf cart, it didn't take me long to get to the scene. As I headed to the beach, I had to walk across the boardwalk over the dunes. The boardwalk was required because it is illegal to walk on the dunes. Human foot traffic would destroy the nesting gopher tortoises. As I walked along the boardwalk, it rose and fell with the contours of the dunes. My emotions were rising and falling in a far more extreme manner than the contours of the dunes. I was excited to finally put my years of training to use, but I was terrified that I would screw it up.

As I came over the last steps of the boardwalk, I saw Officer Stitt struggling to keep curious onlookers from taking pics of the body.

I screamed, "Hey! Everyone who is not in a police uniform needs to go back to their homes, or you will be arrested for interfering with a police investigation."

It did the trick. The crowd immediately dispersed.

"Have you checked him for identification?" I asked Officer Stitt.

"No, you told me not to touch the body," he replied.

"Thank you for doing what I said." I chuckled.

We stood over the body, staring at it for a few minutes.

"He looks to be wearing expensive clothes," Officer Stitt said.

"Yeah, but there are a lot of rich people who live and vacation on this island, so that doesn't help us much." I continued, "Okay, let's check the body together. Put on your gloves."

We gently rolled the body over on his stomach, and I searched the man's back pocket. His wallet was still in his back pocket, and there was over two thousand dollars in cash. It must not have been a robbery gone bad.

"Oh, shit, he has a Department of Justice identification card. Deputy Attorney General Raymond White."

CHAPTER 34

Kelly White

"Yes, I would like to report a missing person. I woke up this morning and couldn't find him on the boat that we are staying on.

"I don't know exactly when he went missing. He had been drinking all day yesterday, so I went to bed without him. I figured that he had passed out somewhere on the boat. I wasn't worried. He often passes out before he comes to bed with me, but when I couldn't find him on the boat this morning, I became very worried.

"His name? His name is Raymond White.

"What? Oh my god, no! It can't be true. Are you sure that it's him?"

I couldn't talk anymore. I began to cry. Theron took the phone.

"Ma'am, this is Dr. Theron Mason. Kelly—I mean, Mrs. White can no longer speak. Do you mind telling me what you told Mrs. White that made her so distraught?

"Damn. Poor Kelly! Okay, we are on the boat *Nomism's*. We are anchored about a half mile off Cape Fear, but I can be at the marina in two hours, and the chief can talk to Kelly then."

As Theron guided the boat to the marina, my other friends gathered around me to lend me emotional support. I really did have the best friends anyone could ask for.

When we docked at the marina, the chief of police and his deputy were there to greet us. With the chief was a team from the Brunswick County Sheriff's Office. Theron invited them on board and granted the team access to search the boat for blood or any other physical evidence. They asked to see our cabin and search Raymond's things. They asked me if they could take his computer.

I didn't know what was on his computer, so I said, "No, I'd rather not give you his computer."

They said okay, but they suddenly became suspicious of me. Their countenance changed immediately.

"Do you have a room on this massive boat that we could talk?" they asked me.

Theron intervened, "Do you really have to talk to her now? She just lost her husband."

"I'm afraid so. Since Raymond White was the number two man at DOJ and died in a suspicious manner, you can be sure that the FBI will be here in the coming days. We want to be able to give them as much information as possible when they do arrive. Now we can either talk here on the boat or escort Mrs. White to the police station and question her there."

"Wait, what do you mean 'suspicious manner'?" asked Ben.

"We'll get to that later," replied Chief Denton. "Right now, we need to talk to Mrs. White."

Theron escorted Chief Denton, Officer Stitt, and me to the small saloon. They began by asking me questions about how Raymond and I met, where we lived, and how long we had been married. Their questions then turned a little more hostile.

"When did you last see your husband?"

"I told Raymond that I was getting a little seasick about eight thirty and went to the lower level of the boat. I took some Dramamine and talked to Tommy for a while before I went to bed."

"Who is Tommy?"

"Tommy is the young man who helps Theron—I mean, Dr. Mason—with the boat. I don't know what his title is, but he does whatever Dr. Mason asks him to do."

"What is Tommy's last name?"

"I don't know."

"Did you and Mr. White have a good marriage?"

"It wasn't a perfect marriage by any means, but I did love him."

"Did he have any enemies on the boat?"

"The people on the boat are my old college friends. They only met him for the first time three days ago."

Chief Denton stood up and walked behind me. "You didn't answer my question. I know a lot of people who can make enemies within three days. I'll ask you again. Was there anyone on the boat who didn't like him?"

"Honestly, Chief Denton, I don't know how my friends felt about Raymond."

"Well, Mrs. White, if he had no enemies on the boat, can you explain to me how he received a contusion on his head?"

He could tell that I was nervous. I was sweating, and I couldn't make eye contact with him. I had nothing to hide, but I didn't want to get my friends in trouble by saying the wrong thing. I remained silent as I thought of how best to answer his question. Silence was not a good strategy.

Chief Denton raised his voice. "Mrs. White, we suspect that your husband was murdered on this boat. If you don't give us any other information, then you will become our chief suspect."

"Murder suspect? Why do you think he was murdered? He was drunk and must have fallen overboard. I don't think anyone on this boat is capable of murdering my husband."

"We will get a toxicological report to see how much, if any, alcohol he had in his system, but he was in good shape. He was a respected DOJ official. It is hard to believe that he was so drunk that he fell over the railing of a boat and then couldn't swim his way back to the boat."

I said nothing.

So Chief Denton continued, "He also had that contusion on his head, which suggests that he was hit over the head and then dumped overboard while unconscious. We will be doing a lot more testing, but right now, it seems pretty clear that he didn't die by accident." He went on, "I will ask you again. How did your husband get that contusion on his head? Don't lie to me, Mrs. White. Lying will only make your situation more tenuous."

"Okay, I will tell you how his head was wounded, but it had nothing to do with his death. On Sunday night, Raymond was again drunk, and he began to sexually assault my friend Sophie. She grabbed an empty wine bottle that was left on the deck and hit him over the head with it. She then ran to her room. Raymond was fine. He had a bandage on his head the next day, but he was not injured."

The chief's curiosity was piqued. He asked me, "So I guess you were pretty angry at Mr. White for coming onto your friend."

"Um, I think I want a lawyer. I didn't kill my husband, but I want a lawyer because you are twisting my words."

"Okay, we won't ask you any further questions until you have a lawyer present, but I am going to insist that you go to your cabin and stay there until we have interviewed your friends."

CHAPTER 35

Sophie Simmons

I was scared. I had never had a speeding ticket much less been interviewed by a police chief regarding the death of someone.

Jed tried to calm me down. "You've done nothing wrong. There's nothing to worry about. I'm going to be there with you as your attorney. If they start asking questions that are outside of the scope of a fact-finding inquiry, I will shut the interview down. You just tell the truth but only answer their question. Do not expound on any answer. Only tell them the minimum necessary to answer the question."

Though I know he was trying to calm me down, his instructions made me even more nervous. I had heard him discuss enough cases to know that our criminal justice system had little interest in justice. They merely wanted to close cases and make headlines about their successful prosecutions.

Chief Walter Denton looked to be in his midfifties. He had a healthy head of gray hair and a chiseled look. His skin looked like he enjoyed the beach's sun. He had what appeared to be a permanent tan and the deep wrinkles that are the price God requires of anyone who enjoys the sun too much.

"Ms. Sophie Simmons?"

I felt like I was in a doctor's waiting room and my name had just been called for a very painful and invasive procedure. I stood up and walked toward Chief Denton. Jed followed me.

"I'm sorry, sir. We just want to interview Ms. Simmons right now. We will get to you later. What is your name?"

"I'm Jed Cummins. I am Ms. Simmons's attorney and will be present during your interview of Ms. Simmons."

Chief Denton looked irritated. "Ms. Simmons, why would you think you need a lawyer for a simple interview?"

Before I could answer, Jed chimed in, "Don't play that game, Chief. Everybody, regardless of their innocence, should have legal counsel present when discussing a possible criminal matter with law enforcement. It is after all their constitutional right. I'll turn your question around. Why would you prefer that she not have an attorney present as you interview her?"

I had never loved Jed more than I did in that moment.

The chief looked defeated, but he quickly rallied. "Mr. Cummins, you were on the boat last night as well, weren't you?"

"I was," said Jed.

The chief said smugly, "Then you are a witness as well, and as I recall, courts prohibit a witness from providing legal representation to another witness. I'm afraid that, if Ms. Simmons wants an attorney present, she will have to find one who wasn't on the boat last night."

It was a gut punch. I did not want to sit through an interview with the police without Jed. I looked at him with fear in my eyes.

He squeezed my hand and said, "Chief, Rule 3.7, known as the advocate-witness rule, prohibits a lawyer from acting as an advocate *at trial* if the lawyer is likely to be a necessary witness. This is not a trial. I am perfectly able to represent Sophie during an interview. Moreover, there is no reason to believe that Sophie or anyone else on this boat would ever be on trial or that I would be a necessary witness at any such imagined trial."

The chief and his deputy turned and whispered to each other for a few moments.

"Fine, Ms. Simmons, you may have Mr. Cummins present during your interview."

I was relieved but still terrified as I followed Chief Denton to the small saloon, which he had commandeered and converted into his interrogation room.

He began by asking me about my past and my previous marriage. I felt like it was invasive and unnecessary. But Jed didn't object, so I answered his questions. The chief then asked me a question that stopped my heart for a moment.

"Ms. Simmons, did you ever have any negative interactions with Raymond White?"

"What do you mean 'negative interactions'?" I replied.

"To be specific, did Raymond White ever sexually assault you?"

Jed looked at me with a look of shock, and I looked at him apologetically.

Jed said, "Chief, I need to talk to my client. Can we take a break?"

The chief stood up to leave the room, saying, "I will give you a break, but I expect an answer to my question when I come back in five minutes."

When the chief came back into the room, he announced a change in the interview itinerary.

"Mr. Cummins, if you are going to sit in on Ms. Simmons's interview, I think I would like to interview you first. Ms. Simmons isn't your attorney now, is she?"

I looked at Jed, confused. He simply nodded to the chief and squeezed my hand, and I left Jed and the chief in the saloon.

CHAPTER 36

Jed Cummins

"Mr. Cummins, I sensed during my questioning of Ms. Simmons that you were taken aback when I asked Ms. Simmons if Mr. White had sexually assaulted her. Did you know that Raymond White sexually assaulted your girlfriend?"

"No, Chief, I didn't know that Raymond White had assaulted Sophie. But you are wrong if you think that his assault of Sophie had anything to do with Raymond White's death."

"When did you find out about the assault?"

"Be careful, Chief Denton. That question violates Ms. Simmons attorney-client privilege. However, she instructed me to answer that question, so with her waiver, I will tell you that I found out five minutes ago, when you left the room so I could consult with my client."

"What did she tell you happened?"

"Again, with her permission, I will tell you what she told me. She said that, on Sunday night, she went to the deck to get some air believing everyone else to be asleep. While she was on the deck, Raymond White approached her. He was drunk. He tried to kiss her and made inappropriate comments. She believed that he intended to rape her. She tried to escape his embrace but couldn't, so she grabbed an empty bottle of wine and hit him over the head with it. He was stunned long enough for her to escape and return to her cabin, where she locked the door. He was never unconscious. She could hear him coming downstairs and returning to his cabin. The next morning, he had a bandage on his head. There were no other interactions between Raymond White and Sophie for the remainder of the trip."

"What would you have done if you had known of Mr. White's assault on Ms. Simmons?"

"I don't know. I may have punched him in the face, but I wouldn't have killed him. I may have called the police and reported his crime, but I'm not sure if it would have done any good," I said rather accusingly.

"Had you ever met Mr. White or known him before arriving on the boat?"

"I am an attorney, so I was aware of who Deputy Attorney General Raymond White was, but I have never met him before I arrived on the boat. I didn't know that he would be on this trip until I got on the boat, and even then, it took several hours for me to realize that he was the same Raymond White."

"Did you have any reason to want Mr. White dead?"

"Of course not."

"When did you last see Mr. White?"

"Last night. Sophie and I saw Raymond in the galley getting a new bottle of scotch as we went to the back deck of the boat for a little quiet time together."

"What time of the night was this?"

"About 10:00 p.m., maybe ten fifteen."

"What kind of condition was he in?"

"Well, we didn't stop to talk to him since we were trying to avoid people so we could have some time to ourselves. But I can tell you that he had been drinking all day, so I suspect that he was pretty blitzed."

"Do you know of anyone on the boat who may have had a reason to kill Mr. White?"

"Chief Denton, I am not saying that I do know of anyone who may have motive to harm Mr. White, but I will tell you that I can't answer questions about the other passengers due to attorney-client privilege."

"Wait, you're telling me that you represent every passenger on this boat?"

"I'm telling you that almost all of them had occasion to solicit my legal opinion on one matter or another."

"Who exactly has sought your legal opinion?"

"Kelly White, Steve Camp, Freedom Goforth, Weston Walker, Ben Eiler, and of course, you know of my representation of Sophie Simmons."

"Mr. Cummins, you have to admit that it is suspicious that almost every guest on this boat has hired you as an attorney within three days of meeting you, and suddenly the deputy attorney general of the United States ends up dead."

"I don't think it is suspicious in the least. We all have problems, Chief. If everyone who has given a lawyer a dollar and asked them for legal advice on the golf course or at a cocktail party were murderers, the crime rate in the United States would be much, much higher. As I said in my previous answer, just because they sought my legal advice does not mean that they disclosed to me a reason to harm Raymond White. It just means that I can't talk to you about them because most everything I know of them was disclosed to me as their attorney."

"Hmm, thank you for your time, Mr. Cummins."

Chief Denton was visibly frustrated with my answers. I asked Chief Denton if he wanted to resume his questioning of Sophie. He said he was going to talk to the others and then, if he needed to talk to Sophie, he would schedule a time.

CHAPTER 37

Ben Eiler

Why would Chief Denton want to talk to me? I barely talked to Raymond all week. I had never had any interactions with the police, and I had hoped to go through the rest of my life maintaining that unblemished record.

"Mr. Eiler, can we talk?"

Well, there goes that record, I thought.

"Sure, Chief Denton."

"When did you last see Mr. White?"

I was surprised with the abruptness of his question.

"I saw him on the front deck as my wife and I headed to our cabin about ten forty-five."

"With my income, I have not been fortunate enough to familiarize myself with thirty-million-dollar yachts, so help me out. What exactly is a cabin?"

I chuckled. "Until this week, I wasn't familiar with yachts either, but I have learned that a cabin is a nautical term for our bedroom."

"Ah, okay, so you and your wife went to bed around ten forty-five?"

"Yes, that is correct."

"Was Mr. White alone when you went to bed?"

"Yes, he was alone. At least I think he was alone. I didn't inspect the entire deck, but I didn't see anyone near him as I went downstairs."

"Did you seek legal advice from Jed Cummins this week?"

"Yes, I did."

"What kind of legal advice were you seeking from him?"

"Well, Chief Denton, that's rather personal, and I don't think I have to answer that due to my attorney-client privilege."

"Well, I'm no lawyer. I'm just a meager police officer, but I believe that attorney-client privilege only protects the conversation between an attorney and their client. So I'll ask again. Without divulging the conversation between you and Mr. Cummins, what was the topic of the conversation?"

"I'm not sure if that's correct, but I'll tell you that the topic of the conversation involved my employment with Coca-Cola."

"That's it? It was about your employment with Coca-Cola?"

"I'm sorry to disappoint you, but yes."

Chief Denton seemed very disappointed with my answer but moved on to ask me how long I had worked at Coca-Cola, what my job duties were there, how Lauren and I had met, and how many kids we had. He was impressed only with the number of kids that Lauren and I had.

CHAPTER 38

Steve Camp

I guess I was next in line. A sharp pain hit my bowels. At first, I wanted to double over in pain. After that feeling subsided, I felt like I was going to vomit at any second. That feeling did not subside so quickly.

Everyone before me had come out of their interview looking haggard, but they all claimed that their interview went okay. Unlike them, though, I was under indictment and awaiting my trial on felony charges. I was scared to death. I wasn't concerned about Raymond's death because I had nothing to do with that. I was, however, very concerned that Chief Denton would end up notifying my pretrial parole officer about my trip and I would spend the next seven months in a county jail awaiting my trial.

"Mr. Camp, tell me about your family. Are you married?"

"Yes, I am married."

"Did your wife accompany you this week?"

"No, she is with the children."

"Was she upset that you got to experience a week on a multimillion-dollar yacht and she had to stay home with the children?"

"To be honest with you, Chief Denton, we are separated. I don't think she would want to spend a week with me even if it were on a multimillion-dollar yacht."

"I'm sorry to hear that, Mr. Camp. I am divorced myself. I know how tough it can be. I have been told that you sought legal advice from Mr. Cummins. Were you asking him advice about your pending divorce?"

"Yes, I have sought advice from Mr. Cummins about my divorce."

"What do you do for a living, Mr. Camp?"

"I was an investment banker, but I am currently taking a hiatus as I look for something else to do with my life."

"An investment banker, you say. I have always wondered what an investment banker does exactly."

I chuckled awkwardly. "Well, we move rich people's money around in different investments, taking a small percentage of their profits until we have enough money to be considered rich like our clients."

"In other words, you tell your clients that two plus two equals five, and you keep the extra one?"

I thought that Chief Denton's characterization of my former profession was completely unfair, but I said, "Yeah, I guess. Something like that."

"Mr. Camp, did you know Raymond White before boarding the boat this week?"

"No, I did not."

"Did you have any encounters with Mr. White while on the boat this week?"

"No, we got really drunk together on the first night and took some shots at each other's profession, but by the next morning, all was forgotten, and we never had a cross word since that first night."

"What exactly did you all say during your drunken stupor?"

"I honestly don't remember. As I said, I was pretty drunk."

"Can you think of anyone on the boat who had a reason to harm Mr. White?"

"Chief Denton, I have known these people since I was in college. I can't imagine any of them harming anyone, especially Kelly's husband."

"When did you last see Raymond White?"

"I had received an email from my estranged wife that upset me. I decided to get drunk in my cabin and fall asleep. I last saw Raymond White in this room—the small parlor—as I grabbed a bottle of Blanton's to take to my room."

"Forgive me. What is Blanton's?"

"I'm sorry. It's a brand of bourbon."

"Gotcha. What time did you last see Mr. White?"

"I retired to my cabin about nine thirty, so I guess it was around 9:25 p.m."

"Okay, last question. What was Mr. White doing when you saw him at nine twenty-five?"

"Well, he was awake, so he was drinking."

CHAPTER 39

Weston Walker

I thought talking to lawyers was bad enough, but now I was having to talk to a chief of police. I thought this little getaway would be a great diversion from the stress of making movies. It had turned out to be a nightmare that no Hollywood producer could script.

"Mr. Walker, you are a movie producer. Is that correct?"

"Yes, it's always disappointing when you meet one in person, isn't it?"

The chief laughed at my often-used joke. "Under different circumstances, I would love to learn more about the movie business and ask you about actors that you have worked with, but right now, I need to ask you about Raymond White's death."

"I understand."

"What legal matter did you discuss with Mr. Cummins?"

"I had a tax question for him."

"A tax question? That seems pretty boring."

"Yes, I'm afraid that the life of a Hollywood movie producer is not as exciting as most people imagine."

"Did you know Mr. White before you arrived on the boat?"

"I didn't know him before I arrived on the boat, and I don't think I know him now. He kept to himself most of the time."

"I'm sensing that," the chief said. The chief continued his inquisition, "Do you know anyone who had a reason to harm Mr. White?"

"No. Like I said, he kept to himself most of the time. I don't think any of us knew him well enough to know if we liked him or disliked him...well, except for Kelly of course."

"When was the last time that you saw Mr. White?"

"Freedom and I saw him around 11:30 p.m."

"Where was he when you saw him?"

"He was on the front deck drinking?"

"Where were you when you saw him?"

"I'm a little embarrassed to tell you. Freedom, my girl-friend, and I thought everyone was asleep, so we snuck to the back of the boat and took a little skinny-dip. By the time we noticed him, he had been watching us in the water for quite a while. We were mortified. We apologized and returned to the back of the boat, swam a little more, and then went to our cabin."

"What did he say when you apologized to him?"

"Nothing. He just nodded."

"Can anyone else verify that you and Ms. Goforth were skinny-dipping around eleven thirty?"

"I certainly hope not."

"When did you go to bed?"

"The clouds moved in and covered the full moon about midnight. It got quite dark and ominous as we floated in the water, so we started swimming toward the boat. By the time we got there, it was a torrential downpour."

"It was raining last night?"

"It rained hard starting about midnight. I don't know how long the rain lasted because we went to bed, but it certainly rained for a while. In fact, it was storming so hard that the boat was rocking to a point that Freedom struggled to climb the ladder back into the boat."

CHAPTER 40

Dr. Theron Mason

Honestly the only good thing that had happened on this trip was the death of Raymond White. Kelly deserved so much better than Raymond. She was an amazing woman whose personality had lay dormant for the last fifteen years because of her now-deceased husband. Yesterday I saw a glimpse of the spark that she used to live every day with. I had nothing to do with Raymond's death, but I couldn't help but celebrate it.

As Chief Denton approached me to begin his inquisition of me, I had an incredible peace. There were no nerves. There was no stress. This wasn't like me. I used to have panic attacks just thinking about my med school exams. Before my first dozen or so surgeries, I would spend twenty minutes puking my guts up. I had suddenly become a Zen master. Hmm, sometimes I fascinated myself.

"Dr. Mason, please have a seat," said Chief Denton. "Did you know Raymond White before you came onto the boat?"

"I did not."

"Did you like him once you did meet him?"

"I did not."

"Why not?"

"I didn't like his personality. I didn't like his bravado. I didn't like how he acted when he was drunk, which was how he spent most of his day. I didn't like how he treated people…especially Kelly. Shall I go on?"

"Well, tell me what you mean about 'how he treated people.'"

"I don't have any specific examples. He was just derisive of people. He belittled Kelly and everyone else whom he encountered. He treated people like they were beneath him."

"Did he treat you the same way, Dr. Mason?"

"Honestly I don't think I ever had one conversation with him. I tried to avoid him, and he never sought me out."

"When was the last time you saw Mr. White?"

"The last time I saw Raymond? I guess it was sometime around 8:30 p.m. I turned in early last night. I don't actually remember seeing Raymond, but I am sure I saw him at some point last night. He just didn't make an impression on me. I was used to seeing him alone with his scotch, so he no longer registered with me."

"Is it possible that a stranger could board the boat after you all went to bed and leave undetected?"

"I guess it's possible. I only turn the security cameras on if we are docked. I never turn them on when we are out to sea because I would never imagine that someone would attempt to board a boat that was a half mile out to sea. However, I guess anything is possible."

"Wait, are you telling me that this boat has security cameras?"

"Yes, but like I said, the system wasn't on last night."

"When was the last time that the cameras were on?"

"I turned the system on yesterday when I went ashore and turned it off when I returned to the boat."

"I want a copy of all the recordings that you have from the time that your friends arrived until last night."

"Okay, I can get it for you right now if you would like."

"Yes, I would like a copy of the video before I leave the boat." As we were walking to the boat's bridge to retrieve the security camera video, Chief Denton asked me, "Dr. Mason, how long are you going to be anchored near the island?"

"We were planning on leaving this coming Sunday. Just one week on the island."

"Well, nobody on this boat is permitted to leave until I say so. I hope I can trust you. If I get word that anyone has left or is planning to leave, I will be forced to detain all of you until all of my questions have been answered."

"Of course, Chief."

After I gave the chief a thumb drive with a copy of the security camera saved on it, Chief Denton looked at his notepad and said, "I have more questions for Ms. Simmons and Ms. Goforth. Is there anyone else on the boat that I haven't questioned?

"There is a sixteen-year-old boy named Tommy. I call him my second mate, but he just helps out around the boat."

"Oh, yes, Tommy. Ms. White mentioned him. I will need to talk to him as well. Unfortunately I must return to the station. We are getting a few test results in soon, and I want to watch this security camera footage, but I will be back tomorrow to finish my interviews."

CHAPTER 41

Chief Walter Denton

As Officer Stitt and I walked down the plank, leaving the yacht, Officer Stitt asked me, "Well, Chief, what do you think?"

"I don't know, Kevin. They disliked him more than they are letting on, but that doesn't mean anyone killed him. Anytime someone is talking to the police, you should expect that they will minimize the truth. Minimizing the truth doesn't mean they are liars, and it certainly doesn't mean that they are murderers. It could mean that they're simply scared. On the other hand, it's possible that they are lying because they did in fact murder Raymond White."

"What do we do now?" asked Officer Stitt.

"Well, first I want to see how much alcohol Raymond White had in his system. Second I want you to call the National Weather Service in Wilmington and see how much rainfall we received last night and the exact time of the rainfall."

"Okay, Chief, will do."

"Then we need to know who these people are. Do a background check on every single person on that boat. Search every database that we have access to. I want to know if they've ever been arrested, how many times they have been married, what their money situation is. Find out everything you can on them. Lastly I want you to research Raymond White. He has been confirmed by the US Senate, which requires a strenuous vetting process, so I doubt that we find anything, but check anyway."

"Yes, Chief."

"Kevin, be discreet when you research Raymond White. I don't want the feds to know that we are investigating the victim."

"Got it."

I needed to clear my head. I was sure that I had missed some things, so I went to get a cup of coffee. One thing I loved about this island was that there were no Starbucks. Instead we had a local coffee shop called Sandpiper Coffee and Ice Cream. Sandpiper is located in the marina district of the Island, just steps from the ferry terminal. Not only is the coffee superior to Starbucks, but it's also locally sourced. They get their coffee from Java Estates Coffee and their ice cream from Coastal Creamery.

"Afternoon, Claire. I'll have an Americana with a triple shot."

"Triple shot, Chief? I'm guessing that body that washed ashore is the reason for the triple shot?"

"I'm afraid so, Claire."

"I know that I shouldn't ask, Chief, but everyone is scared. Was that man murdered?"

"You're right, Claire. You shouldn't ask. But I know everyone is nervous. We haven't had a violent crime on this island since I have been chief, and it's going to be hard to keep people from talking about it. To answer your question, I don't know if he was murdered or if it was just a tragic accident. What I am confident of is that, if it was a murder, Raymond White was the intended victim and nobody else on the island is in danger."

"Oh, Chief, that is such a relief. Do you mind if I assure customers who ask that there is no more danger to worry about?"

"I don't mind," I said though I knew that Claire would tell everyone she knew, not just customers who asked.

I thanked Claire for the triple-shot Americana and headed to a corner table, where I pulled out my laptop, put in my earbuds, and began watching the security camera video that Dr. Mason had provided me. I took my earbuds out when I realized that there was no sound on the footage.

CHAPTER 42

Jed Cummins

After Chief Denton left, I walked around the boat. Everyone looked shell-shocked. It had been a rough morning. First there was the realization that Raymond was missing, then the news that he had died, and then the police interviews.

I asked Theron if he could give Tommy an assignment that would take a while so that the rest of us could meet and decompress. Theron suggested that we all meet on the back deck of the boat. He would give Tommy some work in the engine room that would keep him busy for several hours.

I walked around and asked everyone to join Sophie and me on the back deck. This was a deck that we had never been on. Steve noticed a bar that had been covered to protect it from the rain. He removed the cover to reveal an amazing bar. The under bar appeared to be the fuselage of a small jet; it had the oval windows of a passenger aircraft with soft backlight shining through the passenger windows. The metal was riveted and had a tail number on it—N823SS.

When Theron joined us, Ben asked Theron if it was indeed an aircraft fuselage, and Theron informed us that it was. It was in fact Theron's first jet. He explained that it was a twenty-five-year-old Cessna Citation when he bought it. He had depreciated the jet to zero and didn't want to pay a lot in capital gains tax, so he sold it for scrap but kept a few pieces to decorate his boat and house.

Discussion of the bar was a nice distraction from our otherwise stressful day.

Sophie pulled me aside and whispered, "I don't want any secrets between us. Notice the tail number. My birthday is August 23, 8-23, and SS is obviously my initials. I don't know if it is a coincidence, and I don't want to make a big deal of it. I just wanted you to know."

Wow, Theron really was in love with Sophie. I'm guessing that, if I examined his body, there would be a tattoo of her name somewhere.

Regardless, we had more important things to discuss right now.

Everyone was sitting on the deck. Some had made themselves a drink, and who could blame them after the day that we had had? I stood up and asked for everyone's attention.

I began with an attempt at humor. "Well, that was fun, wasn't it?"

No one laughed though I wasn't expecting a laugh.

I pivoted and asked, "Kelly, how are you feeling?"

"I'm overwhelmed right now. I don't know what I am feeling, exhausted, sad, scared…but also a little relieved to have Raymond out of my life forever."

"That's perfectly normal," I reassured her. "How is everyone else feeling?"

There was silence. No one wanted to answer my question.

Finally Sophie spoke up, "I don't know enough to know how I should be feeling."

Steve followed up on Sophie's statement. "Me too. Jed, tell us what happens next. Tell us what we should expect."

"Okay, I'll do my best, but realize that every investigation is different. First nobody on this boat did anything wrong, so you should take confidence in that. *Most* of the time, our justice system gets it right, but there are certainly examples of when the system gets it *very* wrong, so everyone should remain careful in your dealings with the police."

Steve chimed in, "I can attest to the fact that the justice system gets it wrong."

I placed my hand on Steve's shoulder and continued, "Right now, the chief is waiting for the toxicology report, which we all know will show Raymond to have been highly intoxicated. I'm sure the chief is conducting background checks on all of us."

"Wait," said Steve. "He's doing a background check on us? He will find out that I am under indictment and here without my parole officer's permission."

"Yeah, Steve. I'm afraid that secret is going to be out of the bag."

"I'm fucked then," Steve whispered as he hung his head.

"You have emails and voice mails that show you attempted to contact your parole officer." "Without Raymond pushing the judge to hammer you, you should be fine. The judge may impose a few extra restrictions, but I can't imagine the judge incarcerating you until your trial."

"Really?" asked Steve. "How confident are you that I won't have to go to jail, Jed?"

Again I put my hand on Steve's shoulder. "I'm fairly confident, but let's talk later—when we can talk alone."

I wanted to talk to Steve in private for two reasons. First I didn't want to waste everyone else's time. Second, for attorney-client privilege to attach, the conversation had to be had exclusively between the attorney and the client. Having this conversation in front of everyone would defeat the privilege that Steve might need in the future.

"Chief Denton told Theron that he intends to come back to the boat to conduct more interviews. He will probably have the results of the toxicological results and our background checks completed before he questions us again—"

Theron interrupted me, "And have watched the security camera video."

"You've been video recording us?" asked Weston.

"No," said Theron. "I only turn on the security cameras when we are docked at the harbor and I leave the boat."

"Hmm, so it should have recorded Raymond drinking on the boat all day yesterday?" I asked.

"I guess so," said Theron.

"That's not a bad thing," I said. I continued on, "We should also be prepared for another round of questions, this time from the FBI. I can't imagine that the FBI won't investigate the death of the United States deputy attorney general."

"You've got to be shitting me," said Ben. "This trip is becoming a nightmare."

"What do you mean 'becoming'? It's been a nightmare for quite some time," said Theron.

Sophie, always the optimist, chimed in, "I know it's been a nightmare, and tomorrow the nightmare will resume, but tonight we have great friends, plenty of wine, lots of leftover food. Let's try to talk about other things than Raymond's death and enjoy the night."

CHAPTER 43

Wednesday Night

"Tommy, we're going to be on the back deck tonight. Would you mind bringing some bottles of wine, scotch, and vodka to the back deck bar?"

Dr. Mason didn't order me to stock the bar. Instead he asked me if I "would mind" stocking the bar. That was not like him. He seemed happier than he had all week. I was glad. He deserved to be happy.

After stocking the bar, I poured myself a scotch, which had become my drink of choice after Mr. Cummins introduced it to me. I took my perch on the promenade deck and listened to the conversation. The night was sticky, but otherwise it was a perfect night. The high tide seemed higher than usual. On the horizon, you could see the lights of shrimp boats ending their day and cargo ships waiting for the sun to rise so they could come into harbor. The full moon was especially bright, but it had a unique blue coloring tonight. It was strange how the night could be so perfect when the day was so tragic. I'd like to think God had given these friends the gift of a perfect night to let them know that everything would be okay—but I had my doubts.

Mr. Eiler was a great storyteller. He regaled everyone with an adventure that he, Dr. Mason, and Mr. Camp had in college.

"We were blessed to have a group of friends who all shared a healthy sense of adventure. Instead of spending our weekends bouncing from one fraternity party to the next, we would spend the week planning the next weekend's adventure. One weekend, Ben, Theron, and I decided to make a homemade raft out of wooden pallets and tractor tire inner tubes and float the Broad River, a river renowned for its smallmouth bass fishing. The river originates in the Blue Ridge Mountains of North Carolina. This was a river that we knew well. At least once a month, we found ourselves standing in the Broad River, regardless of the weather, fly-fishing for smallmouth bass.

"Our plan for this adventure was to launch our homemade raft below the dam of Lake Lure and spend the weekend floating to a location below the swinging bridge, where our car would be waiting for us. We were very confident fishermen, so we boldly decided that we would bring only a bag of potatoes and survive off our fishing prowess to feed us for the weekend.

"Nothing went right that weekend. As soon as we launched our raft, the dam ceased to generate water, which meant that there was no flow. We were on a homemade barge with no current. Moreover, though the temperature when we launched our raft was in the nineties, we were unaware that, at night, on an ice-cold river, the temperature would drop to the midforties. Our Umbro shorts and cotton T-shirts were no match for the cold, and of course, as you can anticipate, we caught zero fish all weekend."

Mr. Camp's story was interrupted with laughter from everyone else, including me as I quietly watched from my hidden perch. The story got better.

"On the first night of our adventure, we were huddled together trying to keep warm in the pitch blackness when we heard gunshots. There was splashing near our raft as bullets hit right next to our raft. We immediately forgot how cold we were and began to yell to the 'shooter,' whom we presumed to be on the bank, 'What do you want with us? Please stop shooting at us.' We were terrified.

"Mercifully, during the midst of this life-and-death situation, we rounded a bend in the river and saw an elderly man fishing off his dock. It was a very odd scene to behold, not only because this man was fishing at 3:00 a.m. in the morning, but he also had a pet raccoon sitting on his shoulder while he fished. We began to yell for help as we paddled over to his dock. We were disgusted to see that he did not seem to care about our near-death experience. As we approached the dock, we asked him to call 911. He finally acknowledged us and told us to calm down. He said that he had heard our screams and then informed us that no one was shooting at us. The 'gunshots' that we heard were beavers swimming across the river slapping their tails on the river, and the splashes of water were a result of the beavers' tail slaps, not bullets hitting near our raft.

"We've had many embarrassing moments, but that may have been the most embarrassing."

Everyone loved the story, especially Mr. Cummins. He went on to tell a story on himself, and soon everyone was telling stories and laughing. I was glad they had a good night because it might be the last good night they had in a while.

CHAPTER 44

Dr. Theron Mason

It had been a long and stressful day. I expected to fall asleep as soon as my head hit the pillow. I had miscalculated. I couldn't sleep because my mind was racing—not about the day's events—but about Kelly. I hated myself for contemplating a romantic future with Kelly. Her husband had just died, I should be feeling sympathy for her loss, not plotting my future with her. What's wrong with me? On Sunday night, I had expressed my undying love for Sophie. When she rejected me, I thought that I would never love again. Three nights later, I can't stop thinking about Kelly. The heart is certainly fragile but it can also be very resilient.

Someone knocked at my cabin door. I got up, put on some pajama pants, and opened it. There was Kelly. "Oh, hi. Come on in," I whispered. Before I closed the door, I looked down the hallway to see if anyone had witnessed Kelly entering my cabin. I saw no one and closed the door quickly.

Kelly was wearing a loose-fitting scoop neck *Aerosmith* T-shirt and a pair of high-cut gym shorts. She managed to look both sexy and vulnerable.

"I'm sorry to bother you, Theron. I just don't want to be alone tonight. I hated Raymond but it is still very sad to lay in that big cabin all by myself, knowing that my husband will never climb into bed with me again."

"I understand," I said as I reached over to grab my T-shirt that was laying on a nearby chair. Kelly was crying so I put my T-shirt on—there would be no seducing her tonight. After I had my T-shirt on, I hugged her, and I said nothing—how do you console someone who has lost their husband.

After a few moments, she pulled away from me, wiped tears from her eyes, and sat down on my bed.

"Do you want to talk about it? I asked.

"Not really," she said as she slipped underneath the covers. "I just want to go to sleep."

I wasn't sure what was expected of me. I looked around, there was no couch for me to sleep on, so I walked around to the other side of the bed and climbed in as well. I reached over and turned off the switch to the lights that were ensconced in the headboard.

I laid there in darkness, staring at the ceiling.

"Hold me," Kelly whispered.

I rolled over and laid my arm over her waist. I was careful to leave some distance between our bodies. There was no need to be careful. Kelly backed her body into mine. She felt amazing in my arms. Our bodies fit together like puzzle pieces.

I was trying my best to not get aroused—this was my friend—my friend who was recently widowed. I couldn't control myself. How embarrassing. She had to feel the stiffness in my pajama pants.

I whispered, "I'm sorry. I can't help it."

"Don't apologize," she said as she backed up even closer to me and wiggled her ass until I was pressing against her backside.

She grabbed my arm and pulled me even closer to her. When she felt sufficiently enveloped by me, she went to sleep.

I laid there smelling her hair for another twenty minutes before I dozed off.

At 6:00 a.m., I awoke to Kelly moving gently around the cabin.

"Theron, I'm going to go back to my room. I would prefer people not know that I spent the first night as a widow in your bed."

I nodded. "Of course," I said.

"Thank you, though. I couldn't have survived that first night without you," she said.

She cracked the door open and peeked down the hallway. Apparently, it was all clear. She opened the door, turned back to look at me, gave me a smile, and left the room.

CHAPTER 45

Chief Walter Denton

Thursday—

I had stayed up late last night, watching the security camera footage that Dr. Mason had provided me. I asked Detective Stitt to meet me for coffee on my back porch to develop a plan for the day.

"Chief, this is a beautiful view you have here."

"Thank you," I said. "The house isn't much, but the ocean view is as good as anywhere in the world. Not bad for a local cop."

After serving Detective Stitt some coffee, I got down to business.

"Okay, the toxicology reports show that Raymond White had a .24 blood alcohol level. He was extremely intoxicated."

"So he must have fallen overboard and was too drunk to swim back to the boat?" asked Detective Stitt.

"Perhaps," I said, "but it could also mean that he was so intoxicated that anyone on that boat—including the women—could overpower him and throw him over the railing." I asked, "Did it storm last night?"

"Yes," Detective Stitt responded. "It rained one-half inch from midnight to about 1:30 a.m."

"Did the sheriff's office find any physical evidence?"

"Yes," the detective responded. "They found some of Raymond White's blood on the front deck, but they said that it had been there for a couple of days, which corresponds with Sophie's story of hitting Raymond White on Sunday night after he attempted to kiss her."

We drank our coffee for a few minutes until Officer Stitt asked, "What did the security camera video show?

"Well, it mostly showed Raymond White walking around the boat alone and drinking. But there was one interesting thing. Right before Kelly White left the boat that morning, she and Raymond were in the midst of a rambunctious fight."

"What were they fighting about?"

"I don't know. The video has no sound, but the other interesting thing was that Kelly White and Dr. Mason hugged each other and then left the boat together. It appeared that they were having an intimate conversation as they left."

"Really?" said Detective Stitt. "So you think Kelly White and Dr. Mason are having an affair?"

"I don't know, but it's worth exploring. That would certainly create a motive. Did you find anything interesting in your background checks?"

"Not really. There was one thing. Steve Camp is under federal indictment for insider trading in the Eastern District of New York. I called his parole officer to see if he had any violence in his past, which he doesn't. But his PO didn't know that he had left New York, much less was on a boat off the shore of Bald Head Island."

"Hmm," I sighed.

"I wonder if Raymond White knew that Steve Camp had violated the terms of his release?" Captain Stitt queried.

"Let's go find out."

Chapter 46

Officer Kevin Stitt

I had never been part of a murder investigation. The most violent crime that I had ever investigated on Bald Head was when a drunk vacationer got into a fight with his brother. There was a broken nose and some broken furniture, but by morning, they were laughing with each other and refused to press charges. This case was my opportunity to impress Chief Denton and the FBI, who was scheduled to arrive tomorrow. I had always wanted to be an FBI agent. If I made a good impression on these agents, maybe they would put in a good word for me. I'd already discovered the biggest clue that we had so far—Steve Camp was on the island in violation of the terms of his parole, and it was probable that Raymond White became aware of that.

I asked Chief Denton if I could sit in on the interviews today, and he agreed. I wasn't allowed to speak, but he said that I could write him notes if there were questions that I thought he should ask. I hate to admit it, but I was positively giddy about today.

"Mr. Camp, thank you for your willingness to talk to us again. I think you have met Officer Stitt. He will be joining me for today's interviews."

"Okay."

"Now, Mr. Camp, why did you lie to us yesterday?"

"I didn't lie to you."

"You said—and I'm reading from my notes—that you sought Mr. Cummins's legal advice in relation to your pending divorce. That's not true, is it? You sought his advice about your unauthorized trip in violation of the terms of your parole, didn't you?"

"I didn't lie. You asked, 'I have been told that you sought legal advice from Mr. Cummins. Were you asking him advice about your pending divorce?' I said that I had sought legal advice from Mr. Cummins about my pending divorce, which I had. If you had asked me if I had any other reason to seek legal advice from Mr. Cummins, I would have told you about my parole officer."

The chief was not happy with his answer. I handed the chief a note.

"Why didn't you just tell us that you had been indicted for felony crimes in New York?"

"Because it's not something that I lead my introductions with. People treat me different when they find out. I certainly didn't want the police to start treating me different."

"I see. Did Raymond White know that you were on the boat in violation of the terms of your parole?"

"Yes, he did."

"What did he say to you?"

"He asked me if my parole officer knew that I had left New York and was on a boat in international waters. I tried to explain that I had sent my parole officer countless emails and attempted to call him numerous times to ask him if I could go on this trip. My PO never responded to any of my emails or phone messages."

"Was he sympathetic when you explained this to him?"

"No, he said that he would have my parole revoked and send me to jail to await my trial unless I gave him information to indict my former CEO."

"Did that make you mad? Were you scared of going to jail?"

"It did make me mad and scare me until I talked to Mr. Cummins, who said that it is unlikely that the judge would put me in jail since I have emails showing that I did seek permission to go on this trip."

"Did you want Raymond White dead?"

"Of course not. His death has only complicated matters for me in New York. I wish to God that he was still here and I wasn't having to talk to you all."

"Did you ever have a physical altercation with Mr. White?"

"No, I did not."

"Okay, thank you for your time."

When Mr. Camp left the small saloon, the chief said that he didn't think Mr. Camp was our guy. I was quietly pissed. I wanted Mr. Camp to be the culprit so I could get credit for discovering his motive.

Next up was Dr. Mason.

"Dr. Mason, in watching the security video that you provided us, it appeared to us that Kelly White and her husband were having an intense fight. Do you know what they were fighting about?"

"Not really. They fought the entire time they were on the boat. He treated her terribly, so it could have been anything."

"We noticed that you left the boat with Ms. White immediately following their fight. You gave her a long hug. Are you telling us that she didn't tell you what they were fighting about?"

"She just said he was a jerk. She didn't go into detail."

"Are you having an affair with Kelly White?"

"What? No. I haven't seen Kelly in sixteen years. I actually came on this trip hoping to sweep Sophie off her feet, not Kelly."

There was silence for a while as Chief Denton looked at his notes.

Amid the silence, Dr. Mason added, "If I was trying to hide a relationship or anything, why would I volunteer to give you the security camera video that you didn't even know existed?"

"Okay, I don't have any further questions right now, but nobody is allowed to leave. The FBI is coming tomorrow, and I'm sure they will want to talk to each of you as well."

"Okay," said Dr. Mason.

"Can you ask Tommy to come in? We would like to interview him next."

CHAPTER 47

Tommy

Shit, I didn't know that I would have to talk to the police. I was just a kid. Were there not laws against interviewing kids without their parents present?

When Dr. Mason told me that the chief of police wanted to talk to me, I was frozen. I couldn't take a step. Just then, Mr. Cummins walked by.

"Mr. Cummins, can I ask you a question? The police want to talk to me. I don't want to talk to them. Are they allowed to question a child without my mom there?"

"Every state is a little different. Let me check North Carolina's law." He pulled out his phone and started researching my question. "Okay, here we are. 'Police are free to approach and question any child who may have witnessed or been the victim of a crime just as they can contact and interview an adult. Police can question a child without a parent present and are not required to obtain permission from a parent before questioning the child. However, if a parent is present when the police approach the child or police ask permission in advance, a parent can refuse to allow the child to be interviewed.'"

"What does that mean?" I asked.

"Well, if you can get a hold of your mom in the next five minutes, she can tell the police that she is refusing to allow them to talk to you without her present."

"My mom's workplace won't allow her to have a phone with her while she is working. There's no way that I can get a hold of her in the next five minutes. Mr. Cummins, can I hire you to go in there with me?"

"I'm afraid not, Tommy. First there is a potential conflict in me representing you and Sophie though you both could acknowledge and waive any potential conflicts of interest. The bigger issue is that you are a minor, and you aren't old enough to contractually hire a lawyer. Your mom could hire me to represent you, but you can't get a hold of her. I'm afraid that you are going to have to do this interview alone. We can talk to your mom when she gets off work, and you won't have to do any more interviews, but I think this one is unavoidable."

"It sucks to be a kid. I don't want to talk to the police. I certainly don't want to talk to the police without my mom telling me it's going to be okay."

*****

"Tommy, thank you for talking to us."

"Do I have a choice?" I asked.

"No, I guess you don't."

The chief questioned me about how I got my job with Dr. Mason. He asked me if I knew anyone other than Dr. Mason before they arrived on the boat. I said that I did not.

"When did you last see Raymond White?"

"I don't know when it was. Maybe eight. I went to bed early."

"Why did you go to bed so early? You're a young man on a huge boat off the coast of a stunning island. I'm surprised that you would choose to go to bed so early in the evening."

I didn't say anything for a while as I thought about my answer.

"Tommy, don't lie to me. If you lie to me, I can charge you with impeding an investigation."

"I went to bed early because I had been drinking scotch. I am not used to drinking, and it hit me suddenly. I was going to be sick, so I went to my bedroom."

"Scotch? That's a heavy drink to start with. Did someone give you the scotch?"

"Mr. Cummins gave me some of his and told me not to tell anyone. After my first drink, I began to pour myself my own scotch."

"Tommy, you know that, as a minor, you should not be drinking alcohol, don't you?"

"Yes, sir."

"I could charge you with minor in possession, but if you tell me the truth and tell me everything that you have seen and heard while you have been on this boat, I will let you go this time."

"Thank you, sir. I will tell you everything I know."

"Okay, Tommy, tell me. Did everyone get along with Raymond White?"

"No, sir. The only one who would talk to him was Mr. Cummins, but you have to understand. Mr. White was an asshole—Sorry, I should say he was a jerk to everyone, so you can't blame them for not liking him."

"You can say asshole. So how was he an asshole to everyone?"

"Well, I heard a conversation where Mr. Camp told Mr. Cummins that Raymond White had confronted Mr. Camp about skipping bail. He said that he would make Mr. Camp go to jail to await his trial unless he gave him information that would allow Mr. White to indict Mr. Camp's CEO."

Chief Denton and Officer Stitt were writing feverishly as I talked.

Chief Denton didn't look up from his note-taking but said, "Go on."

"That same night, Ms. Freedom and Mr. Walker told Mr. Cummins that Raymond White had told Mr. Walker that he would charge him with tax evasion unless Mr. Walker made a movie about Raymond White."

"Did Mr. Camp and Mr. Walker seem upset?"

"Of course. Wouldn't you be upset if someone was threatening to ruin your life?"

"Yes, I guess I would be. What did Mr. Cummins say after hearing of these stories about Mr. White?"

"He tried to defend Mr. White. He said that he was drunk when he made these threats. He asked them if Mr. White had said anything to them since the initial conversation. Mr. Camp and Mr. Walker said that he had not. Mr. Cummins said that he was sure that it was just the rantings of a drunk man and they shouldn't be worried."

"Did Mr. Camp and Mr. Walker accept Mr. Cummins' explanation?"

"I don't really know about Mr. Camp and Mr. Walker, but Ms. Freedom said that Mr. Cummins was wrong about Mr. White."

"Okay, Tommy, you have been very helpful."

"Chief Denton, please don't tell them that I told you about overhearing their conversation. I really like all of them. They are good people, and I don't want them to be mad at me."

"I'll do my best, but I can't promise you that they won't find out. One last question, did you ever see or hear anything that would make you think that Dr. Mason and Mrs. Kelly White were romantic?"

"Nothing until the night that Mr. White disappeared."

"What happened?"

"I was walking back to the galley after dropping anchor, and I saw Dr. Mason and Mrs. Kelly in the hallway. Dr. Mason gave Mrs. Kelly a small kiss and left. It was a very small kiss, like a friend's kiss."

"Friend's kiss? I don't kiss my friends. Do you kiss your friends, Tommy?"

"No, sir, I don't guess I do."

CHAPTER 48

Agent Joshua Bolding

I knew Raymond White well. He was my boss (actually, my boss's boss). He was an aggressive prosecutor. He had brought down an organized crime syndicate and numerous drug cartels. He had survived the scandal of an interoffice indiscretion to have a stellar career at the Department of Justice. He was also a pompous, egomaniacal drunk. He had no qualms about cutting corners, ignoring DOJ protocols, or even ignoring the law if it meant securing a conviction.

I know the average person would be offended by prosecutors who violate the law to convict someone else of violating the law, but they don't understand the pressure that exists to obtain convictions. If they were the victim or the victim's family, they would not object to a prosecutor doing whatever necessary to put the bad guy away.

Raymond White was a prosecutor's prosecutor. He protected his "boys." If a prosecutor's unlawful actions happened to be brought to a judge's attention (which was very rare), Raymond White would protect the prosecutor; and in fact, he would give them a promotion by moving them to DC and hiring them at the Department of Justice to oversee other prosecutors.

Because of that, Raymond had a lot of friends at DOJ. So when he died on some boat off the coast of Bald Head Island, my team was brought in and told to drop everything else and investigate Raymond's boat mates.

My team consisted of me (I was the team leader), Sylvia Batina, and Matt Mitchell. Sylvia was a great agent. She was conscientious and did everything by the book. She began her career in Bismark, North Dakota, and due to her work ethic and unblemished record, she managed to escape Bismark and eventually come to the DC office. Sylvia also had the benefit of being very attractive. It was disconcerting to suspects when a beautiful five-foot-nine blond-haired woman walked in to interrogate them. She often would flirt with a suspect to gain their trust and tell her what she wanted to know. She had a model's body but tried her best to hide it. She was determined to succeed in this "boy's club" using her intellect and instincts. I respected the hell out of her.

Matt was not so unblemished. He came from the Atlanta office. He was a rising star until he was caught withholding evidence in a high-profile white-collar case. In his defense, he only withheld the evidence because he had obtained it unlawfully. The judge in the case agreed with our prosecutors; they did not dismiss the case and only excluded the wrongfully obtained evidence. They did not apply the "fruit of the poisonous tree" doctrine, which would have excluded all evidence that was sought after the unlawful evidence was obtained. Thank God the vast majority of judges in this country bend over backwards to protect the government's cases.

Regardless, Matt was transferred to DC per Raymond White's instruction and assigned to my team. Matt was highly motivated to prove that Raymond was murdered.

We landed in Wilmington, North Carolina; rented a car; and drove to Southport. We arrived late Thursday night, checked in to our hotel, and went straight to bed. It had been a long day, and we were scheduled to meet with the local chief of police on his back porch first thing in the morning—or as early as the ferry could get us to Bald Head Island.

CHAPTER 49

Thursday Night

I felt so bad. I don't believe that anyone hurt Raymond White. The remaining people on the boat were some of the nicest people that I had ever met. Because of me and what I told Chief Denton, one of them might be arrested for murdering Raymond White. I had to tell someone what I had done. The natural person to tell was Jed Cummins.

"Mr. Cummins—"

"Call me Jed, please."

"Okay, Jed, can I talk to you…in private?"

"Absolutely, but first call your mom. Tell her everything that has happened. Ask her if she will send you a text saying that she does not want you to talk to the police anymore without her being present. Also ask her if she will hire me to represent you. The fee will be one dollar, and she can pay me when we meet, but before you tell me anything, I want it protected by attorney-client privilege."

"That's smart," I replied.

My mom was obviously concerned, but I assured her that Raymond White's death was an accident and the police would be done with their investigation soon. Dr. Mason and I would be sailing back to Myrtle Beach in a few days.

"Okay, Mr. Cummins—I mean, Jed, here is the text from my mom."

After looking at the text from my mom, Jed said, "Okay, you are now my client. Anything you tell me is completely confidential. What do you want to talk about?"

"Jed, I feel terrible. The chief of police told me that, if I didn't tell him everything I knew, he would charge me with minor in possession."

"Minor in possession? Did you tell him that you had been drinking?"

"Yes, Mr. Cummins. I am sorry. I also told him that you had given me my first taste of scotch."

Mr. Cummins chuckled and said, "That's fine. If they want to charge me with contributing to the delinquency of a minor, I guess I will have to admit guilt. Go on, Tommy. What else did you tell the police?"

"I told them about Mr. White threatening Mr. Camp and Mr. Walker."

"How did you know about that?" Mr. Cummins asked.

"I was on the promenade deck and overheard you all's conversation. I am so sorry."

"You have nothing to apologize for, Tommy. As your lawyer, let me advise you to always tell the police the truth. Also, as your lawyer, let me advise you to stay off the promenade deck. Overhearing private conversations is what put you in this situation."

"I will spend the rest of this trip in my cabin," I swore.

"Is there anything else that you told the police?" asked Mr. Cummins.

"Yes, I'm afraid so. I told them that I saw Dr. Mason and Mrs. White share a kiss on Tuesday night. I told them that it was a small kiss, but the chief didn't seem to care."

"Wait, you saw Theron and Kelly kiss each other?"

"Yes, sir."

"Wow," said Mr. Cummins. "Okay, you don't say a word about any of this to anyone else. If the police ever want to talk to you again, you come get me. I won't let them talk to you again unless your mom is present. For now, it's probably best if you do your jobs on the boat and keep a low profile the rest of the time, and don't drink any more scotch," he said with a smile.

CHAPTER 50

Jed Cummins

Based on Tommy's statements, the police probably suspected that either Sophie, Steve, Wes, Freedom, Theron,
or Kelly may have been involved in Raymond's death. I'm
sure the police believed that they all had a motive. Luckily
they didn't know about Ben's beef with Raymond, or he
would be added to the suspect list as well. Jeez, what a mess.

"Jed, everyone is scared. They want to talk to you.
Can you come to the small saloon and answer everyone's
questions?"

I was nervous about talking to the entire group. There
were so many conflicts of interest and privilege issues. I
would be navigating a land mine in trying to answer their
questions, but it was Sophie asking me. I couldn't say no
to Sophie.

"Hey, everyone, I know it's been a tough day, but I'm
afraid that tomorrow may be worse."

"Why do you say that?" asked Theron. "What could
make tomorrow worse than today?"

"Okay, before I answer that question, I need you all
to know that to answer your questions may violate some
confidences. I'm not positive that it will because there have
been so many conversations and I can't recall which ones

are privileged and which ones are not. There also may be conflicts. For this conversation, and only this conversation, I need you all to waive privilege and acknowledge and waive any conflicts of interests."

I went around the room; and everyone, including Sophie, waived privilege and conflicts of interest.

"Okay, I know that you are all good people. I know that you all did nothing wrong, but you should know that Chief Denton is aware of Raymond's threat against Steve. He is aware of Raymond's extortion attempt against Weston and Freedom. He is aware of Raymond's attempted rape of Sophie. He is aware of the huge fight that Raymond and Kelly had the morning of Raymond's death. He also suspects that Kelly and Theron are having an affair, which gives Theron motive."

"What?" exclaimed Freedom. "Theron and Kelly having an affair? Why would he think that?"

She wasn't asking me that question. It was directed at Kelly and Theron.

Theron and Kelly looked at each other for a moment before Theron spoke up.

"We are not having an affair. However, after her fight with Raymond, Kelly and I spent the day on the island together. It was a good day. Despite everything going on, I managed to have a wonderful time with Kelly. After returning to the boat, Kelly was understandably scared of dealing with Raymond. I offered her encouragement, told her that she would survive this, and gave her a slight kiss. That's it. That's all that has happened though I will admit to hoping that more will develop between Kelly and I after this dreadful trip concludes."

Kelly blushed and smiled but said nothing.

Sophie said, "Kelly, Theron, I think that is wonderful. You two deserve to be happy, and I think you would be perfect together."

"How did Chief Denton find out about all of our secrets?" asked Freedom.

I couldn't answer Freedom truthfully without violating Tommy's privilege. "It's not important. It may be the video that Theron turned over, or it could be that someone on the boat told them about this information during their interview with the chief."

I shouldn't have said that. Everyone began looking around the room with suspicions of who the traitor was.

"It also could be that no one told them anything," I said. "Instead it could be that Raymond had told someone at the Department of Justice about his research on each of you."

Theron spoke up, "Well, they didn't know about my and Kelly's kiss because of the security camera footage. I was sure to turn off the security cameras as soon as we got back on the boat. Someone in this room saw it and told the police."

Weston was next. "And I can't believe that Raymond would tell someone at the Department of Justice that he was planning on extorting me and Freedom. Why would he do that? I agree with Theron. We have a snitch in the room."

I needed to calm everyone down. "Hang on, every-one. The last thing any of my 'clients' need is for there to be dissension among the ranks. Finger-pointing may get someone unjustly charged with Raymond's murder."

There was silence. I took their silence as acquiescence to my advice.

I went on, "Tomorrow the FBI wants to interview some or all of us. They are probably going to know more about our lives than we know about ourselves. There is no point in trying to figure out who told whom what. There are no secrets when the FBI investigates someone...and know this. We are all being investigated."

I was preaching now.

"Instead of being upset with a possible snitch, focus on what we know. Raymond was very drunk. There was a storm pop-up while Raymond was on the deck. The most logical and likely explanation is that Raymond slipped and fell over the railing and then was too drunk to swim back to the boat. Everything else is just speculation. There may have been a lot of people on this boat who didn't like Raymond and are happy that he is gone, but without any direct evidence, the law should accept the most likely and logical explanation. It was an accident."

"Jed, I am an expert on the subject of how much the DOJ cares about the truth," interjected Steve. "I am not nearly as confident as you are in your speech about 'the truth shall set you free.'"

Steve had a good point.

"I know, Steve, and I don't disagree with your perspec-tive. My point is that they know everything." I looked at

Ben and said, "Or they will know everything. So there's no point to be upset with who is the snitch. You should assume that they know the answer to every question that they ask you. I don't believe any of you murdered Raymond, but if you lie to the FBI, they will charge you for that. They will then promise you leniency if you testify against one of your friends, and then it becomes a circular firing squad."

Ben had been silent so far, so I was surprised when he spoke up.

"Jed, we can't be honest about everything."

I gave him a look of confusion.

Ben turned to his college friends and said, "Guys, I think it's time we tell Jed about Mexico."

CHAPTER 51

Agent Joshua Bolding

Friday—

Most of my investigations took me to places where concrete dominated the landscape. The most scenic thing I typically encountered was the graffiti that underprivileged artists created in their effort to express themselves. This investigation was different. Bald Head Island was like nothing I had ever encountered. Sure, I'd vacationed at all the popular "destination" beaches, but the commercialization of those beaches camouflaged their natural beauty. Bald Head has managed to remain a community—a small community. It's certainly not overcommercialized. In fact, it may be under-commercialized. There's a market, a coffee shop, a couple of private clubs, a hardware store, and a few other stores; but that's it. There are no Starbucks, no chain restaurants, and no beach resorts. I hate that it took Raymond White's death to introduce me to this island, but I would be back. Next time, it would be under better circumstances.

Police work was different on this island. We met the chief of police, a Walter Denton, on his back deck. When Agent Batina, Agent Mitchell, and I arrived at the chief's bungalow, he introduced us to Officer Kevin Stitt and directed us to his back deck, where he had a fresh pot of coffee, coffee mugs, and his files on a wooden table. He instructed us to enjoy the view of the beach while he finished making eggs and bacon for us. I typically had to sooth the egos of local law enforcement. They either resented our meddling in their case or tried too hard to impress us. Chief Denton did neither. He was comfortable in his own skin and content with his life choices. He was happy to be the chief of police for Bald Head Island and seemed competent. He was grateful for our help but not desperate for it.

We compared notes, and I must admit—Chief Denton had uncovered a lot of information during his two-day head start.

"Did you all know Raymond White?" he asked.

"Yes, we had worked with him. Since I've been with the bureau the longest, I knew him the best," I said.

"Was he capable of abusing his position of authority as much as the 'suspects' claim?"

Sylvia (Agent Batina), who had always thought that Raymond White was a bully, responded before I could, "Honestly I wouldn't put it past him."

Chief Denton looked like he was surprised by Sylvia's transparency.

I chimed in, "Well, he was an aggressive prosecutor, but we have no evidence that he ever abused his position." I shot Sylvia a disapproving glance.

Chief Denton then asked, "Was he a drunk?"

"I know that he enjoyed a drink or two, but he never appeared drunk at work. So either he was a casual drinker, or he was the most functional drunk in DOJ history, and believe me, we have had a lot of functional drunks, including some attorney generals."

Chief Denton chuckled.

Now it was my time to ask questions.

"So tell us about these college friends. Do you think one of them is a murderer?"

CHAPTER 52

Dr. Theron Mason

I felt like an injured seal in Gansbaai, South Africa, struggling in the narrow sea channel between Geyser Rock and Dyer Island (known as Shark Alley). I'd been interviewed by Sheriff Denton, but now that my blood was in the water, the FBI had come in to pick my carcass clean.

Agent Bolding looked like the stereotypical FBI agent. He was about six feet tall and had a lean physique with a haircut that was popular in the 1950's—short and parted on the right. The other two agents did not look stereotypical. Agent Batina was atypical because of her beauty and Agent Mitchell because of his beard. Agent Mitchell looked like he belonged on a SWAT team. He had a shaved head, but his beard made up for the lack of hair on his head. He was stout. He looked like he should have been a member of a motorcycle gang rather than a member of an FBI investigative team. I wondered what their first impressions of me were.

They set up the chairs around the small table in the saloon so that all five of them were on one side and I was seated alone on the other side of the table. I'm assuming they did this to intimidate me. If so, it worked.

After asking me about my past and work history, Agent Bolding jumped into the meat of the interview. "Why did you lie to Sheriff Denton about your relationship with Kelly White?"

"I didn't lie to him. I said that I wasn't having an affair with Kelly, and I'm not."

"Dr. Mason, you were seen kissing Mrs. White on the night that Raymond White died. Do you make it a custom to kiss women whom you aren't engaged in a relationship with?"

"No, but I've been friends with Kelly for sixteen years. She had a big fight with her husband that morning. She asked me to go to the island with her. We had a good day. We went to the chapel and prayed. We reconnected after sixteen years. It was special. When we got back to the boat, I told her to be strong. I instinctively gave her a small kiss. There have been no intimate interactions with her since then. I don't consider that a 'relationship,' so I answered Sheriff Denton's question truthfully. If he had asked me whether I had ever kissed Kelly, I would have answered yes."

"Did Kelly White want Raymond White dead?"

"Of course not. She may have wanted a divorce, but she never gave any indication that she wanted her husband dead."

"Where were you at one on Tuesday night? I guess that would actually be Wednesday morning."

"I was in my cabin."

"Were you asleep?"

"I was fading in and out of sleep."

"Can anyone verify that you were in your cabin all night?"

"No, I don't guess so."

"Did you see or hear anything unusual that night?"

"Weston and Freedom's cabin is next to mine. They kept me up Sunday and Monday night with their—well, you know—with their activities. On Tuesday night, though, there were no noises from their bedroom until about twelve thirty or one, when I heard them sneaking into their room."

"Do you think Weston and Freedom murdered Raymond White?"

"I don't think so, but if anyone did, it would be them. They didn't go to their cabin until very late, and Raymond White had threatened to destroy Weston and Freedom if Weston didn't make a movie about his life. Weston couldn't afford to make what would be a terrible movie. I know they were very scared about Raymond White's threats and felt trapped."

"Okay, thank you for telling us that. Last question, Raymond White had been doing some research on all of you. One topic of his research has us intrigued. Do you know why he would be researching the death of General Roderigo Sanchez?"

CHAPTER 53

Freedom Goforth

"Let's get this over with."

That probably wasn't the best way to begin my interview, but I was very angry with the DOJ. The deputy attorney general had tried to extort my boyfriend by threatening him with bogus tax evasion charges, and now the FBI suspected us of murder. I thought, if you treated people right and were kind, you never had to worry about our justice system trying to destroy you. I guess I was naive. Maybe they taught that during my senior year of college—which I had skipped.

They began the interview by asking me the exact same questions that Chief Denton had asked me.

"Do you all compare notes? Because Chief Denton has already asked me the same questions and has all the answers."

"We like to be thorough, Ms. Goforth. Now Dr. Mason told us that you and your boyfriend did not return to your cabin until around 1:00 a.m. on the night of Mr. White's death. That is approximately the time that the medical examiners say that Mr. White died. Can you tell us what you and Mr. Walker were doing so late at night?"

"Theron told you that? What a...Well, he's right. As we told Chief Denton, Weston and I went skinny-dipping that night."

Agent Mitchell jumped in, "Skinny-dipping? Does that mean you went swimming naked?"

I don't know why, but the way he said naked gave me the creeps. He was looking me up and down as he said it.

"Yes," I said, "that's what skinny-dipping means. My boyfriend and I swam naked. Is that a crime?"

"No," said Agent Mitchell. "But it was cloudy night with a storm approaching. Doesn't seem like a great night to get naked and jump into the ocean."

"Every night is a good night to get naked with Weston, Agent Mitchell." I took some satisfaction in making Agent Mitchell blush.

"Did anyone see you swimming naked in the ocean?" asked Agent Mitchell.

"As we told Chief Denton, we swam around to the front of the boat, where Raymond was drinking on the front deck. We eventually noticed that he was watching us. We were embarrassed, so we swam to the back of the boat and enjoyed each other's company for a while longer."

"Did anyone who is still alive see you?" asked Agent Mitchell.

"Not that I know of."

Agent Bolding resumed the interview, "What time did you return to your cabin?"

"I think we returned to the cabin about twelve thirty. You can check because we came in as soon as it started raining. I'm sure you can determine when it began to rain.

I can't believe Theron acted like that there was something sinister about us coming to our cabin late."

They were checking their notes for their next question. My blood was boiling.

I couldn't believe Theron would say that. I couldn't stay quiet any longer. "If you want to know about some suspicious behavior, let me tell you about Theron. Every night that we have been on this boat, Theron's room has been as quiet as a church mouse. He goes to his cabin, and he goes to bed…except that night. When we went to our cabin after skinny-dipping, we could hear him moving around his cabin. Either there was someone in his cabin with him, or he was getting dressed or undressed or something. He was certainly not sleeping like he has every other night."

"Okay, thank you for telling us that. We've been told that Raymond White had threatened to prosecute your boyfriend for tax evasion. Is that true?

"Yes, though Weston did nothing wrong."

"Did that scare you and Mr. Walker?"

"Well, it wasn't pleasant, but Weston talked to his attorney and was assured that he had done nothing wrong."

"Are you glad that Raymond White is dead?"

"No, his death has caused all of this insanity. I wish he was still alive and we were able to finish our vacation in peace."

"Do you know why Raymond White was researching the death of a Mexican general named Roderigo Sanchez?"

"I have never heard that name before."

CHAPTER 54

Kelly White

None of us have to be perfect. I certainly hadn't been, but we do have to be aware of our own shit. The last thing I said to my husband before he died was that I hated him and wanted a divorce. As much as I had grown to despise Raymond, I would forever be haunted by my last words to him. I had such hope and excitement when I first met Raymond. I envisioned a wonderful marriage, a happy home full of children, and Raymond and I attending galas together on DC's Embassy Row. I wasn't grieving the death of Raymond, but I was grieving the end of my marriage and the end of the dream.

I now had to recreate who I was, find a new dream, and commit myself to healing. Unfortunately that process would have to wait. My immediate task was to convince Chief Denton and the FBI that I had nothing to do with Raymond's death.

After the three FBI agents introduced themselves to me, they repeated the same questions that Chief Denton had asked me: name, address, and occupation.

Agent Bolding then asked me, "Are you married?"

I stared at him.

He quickly realized his mistake and apologized profusely. "Mrs. White, I am so sorry. I have done thousands of these interviews, and I ask the same first five questions in every interview. It's no excuse, but habit took over. Forgive me. I know that your husband died and his death is the reason that we are here. Again forgive me for being so insensitive."

"It's fine, Agent Bolding. I understand."

"Okay, let's take a break for a few minutes," Agent Bolding said as he and his agents got up and left the room. When they came back, Agent Sylvia Batina took over the questioning of me. My guess is that Agent Bolding recognized that it would be difficult for him to be my interrogator after his gaffe.

"Mrs. White, we have heard from your friends that, on the morning of his death, you had told Mr. White that you wanted a divorce. Is that true?"

"Yes, it is."

"What was his response?"

"He said that he wouldn't let me divorce him."

"How could he stop you from divorcing him?"

"Finances. I haven't had a job since we got married. His wealth was amassed before we got married. He claims that I would not be entitled to any of that. We have no children, so I wouldn't even get child support."

"Is he right about the finances?"

"Yes, I believe he is. I finally reached the point that I didn't care. I was going to divorce him anyway."

"But now that he is dead, you inherit his wealth, don't you?"

"I don't know. I don't know if he even has a will, and if he does, I don't know what's in it."

"What happened that made you declare to Mr. White that you were going to divorce him? I mean, you and Mr. White were together on a beautiful boat off the coast of a beautiful island. Why announce your divorce here? Why now?"

"I guess it was the encouragement of my friends. They saw how he treated me and gave me the strength to do what I should have done years ago."

"Let's talk about your friends. In particular, let's talk about one of your friends, Dr. Theron Mason. Are you and he romantically involved?"

"No, we had one sweet day together—"

"The day your husband died?" Agent Betina said sarcastically.

"Um, yes, it was the day my husband died."

"Go on," Agent Betina said.

"We had a sweet day together. I was distraught from my fight with Raymond. Theron spent the day with me. We prayed in the chapel, shopped, talked. It was sweet. As we came back to the boat, he knew I was nervous about seeing Raymond. He gave me a peck and told me to be strong."

"To be clear, he kissed you on the lips, correct?"

"Yes, a very short peck on the lips."

"You told Chief Denton that you had gone to bed early that night?"

"I did."

"Did you ever leave your cabin that night to visit Dr. Mason?

"I didn't leave my cabin to visit Theron, but I did leave my cabin to go to the restroom. Theron heard someone in the hallway. He thought it may be Tommy trying to sneak a bottle of scotch, so he opened his cabin door. I went into his room for a few minutes and gave him a report on how my night went with Raymond. We hugged, and I returned to my room. I was only in his room for a few minutes."

"What did you say in your report to Dr. Mason about your evening with Raymond?"

"Only that Raymond and I barely spoke. Raymond sat at the bar. The only thing he said to me all night was 'When is dinner going to be ready?'"

"Mrs. White, did you kill your husband so you could inherit his money, or was it so you could be with Dr. Mason?"

"Wait, what? I didn't kill my husband at all. I don't think I will get any of his money, and I do not have romantic feelings for Dr. Mason."

CHAPTER 55

Ben Eiler

I've been questioned and interrogated more on this vacation than my entire life. Chief Denton had questioned me twice, and I was about to be questioned by the FBI. However, the most difficult interrogation came at the hands of my sweet wife, Lauren, when we told Jed, Weston, and Lauren about our Mexico trip. I couldn't be upset with Lauren. It's pretty shocking to receive news that your husband of fourteen years was involved in the death of a Mexican general. She wanted to know every detail. She then began to question whether one of my friends may have been capable of killing Raymond White as well.

I finally said, "We may have killed a man, but none of us are murderers."

After a few more hours of coming to terms with this information, she reached the point of acceptance—followed quickly by defiance. Within a few hours, she had gone from shock and disgust over our actions to defending our actions with every fiber of her being. Our secret was safe with her. Not only was my marriage intact, but it was stronger than ever. Sophie had been right—there shouldn't be secrets in a marriage, certainly not one as big as "I killed someone while I was in college." A wall between Lauren and I that I didn't even know existed had crumbled, and it felt amazing. We were a team, and we had a game plan. Whatever they asked us, Mexico never happened.

"Mr. Eiler, why was Raymond White investigating your hiring at Coca-Cola?"

What? I was expecting questions about Raymond White's death and maybe questions about the death of a Mexican general. I was not expecting questions about my hiring at Coca-Cola. I was hoping that this was just a tactic. They wanted to throw me off by asking me unexpected questions.

Stay calm, Ben. Stay calm.

"I don't know why he would be investigating me at all," I said.

"Well, maybe this will help clarify things for you. Apparently Raymond discovered that you had obtained your high-ranking job at Coca-Cola by diverting federal USAID funds to the company. Does that ring a bell, Mr. Eiler?"

"There was no quid pro quo. The company was entitled to that money per the agency's guidelines, and my hiring was just a result of the fact that they saw my work and were impressed with me."

"Well, there's no point in arguing with you because the statute of limitations has run," said Agent Bolding.

Agent Benita glanced at Agent Bolding and then said, "Additionally Raymond White seems to have obtained your private information without a warrant, so we wouldn't bring the case anyway."

I was taken aback, so I just nodded.

Agent Bolding continued, "While we can't prosecute you for using federal funding to secure yourself a job, we can prosecute you for murder if you killed Raymond White to keep your past a secret. So where were you about 12:30 to 1:00 a.m. on the night Raymond White died?"

"As I told Chief Denton, my wife and I went to bed at ten forty-five. We saw Raymond on the deck drinking as we headed to bed. He was very drunk, but he was very much alive."

"Okay, so do you know why Raymond White was researching the death of Mexican general Roderigo Sanchez?"

"No, I don't know that name."

"Did you and your friends ever take a trip to Mexico?"

"What? Why are you asking me this?"

"Just answer the question."

"No...not really. We went to South Padre Island for a spring break and went across the border to Matamoras, Mexico, to shop, but that's it."

"What was the date of that trip?"

"I don't remember. It was over sixteen years ago."

"You can surely remember what year it was, can't you?"

"I guess it was in 2005."

"Would it have been March 28 to April 5, 2005?"

"I don't know. That sounds about right."

"That was the same week that General Sanchez was murdered."

I was feeling trapped. He was cornering me.

I sat silent for a moment and then said, "There were probably thousands of people who were murdered that week. What's your point?"

"I think you know my point. I think you and your friends know exactly what my point is."

CHAPTER 56

Chief Walter Denton

I had invited my new FBI agent friends over for dinner, not because I was wanting to share a lovely evening dining as we told old war stories. Instead I invited them over because I was pissed and wanted to let them know about it.

"You guys came to my island asking me to 'cooperate' with you. I don't know what the word *cooperate* means in DC, but here it means sharing all information with each other."

They started to defend themselves, but I wasn't done.

"Upon your arrival, I shared every bit of information that I and Officer Stitt had uncovered. You promised to do the same. Yet today you all were asking questions about this General Roderigo Sanchez. Who the hell is General Sanchez, and what does he have to do with this case?"

"I'm sorry, Chief. It wasn't intentional." Agent Mitchell's apology didn't help matters.

"I know it wasn't intentional, Agent Mitchell. That's the problem. You don't consider us partners. You treat us local police as if we were your interns whose job it is to provide coffee and make photocopies. Of course you would forget to tell the interns important matters."

Agent Bolding stepped in, "Chief, you are right. We couldn't conduct this investigation without you, and we have neglected to keep you informed. We have treated you like interns. It's an ongoing problem based on our institutional ego. That's not an excuse. It's just the truth. I promise to not let it happen again."

I nodded.

He continued, "General Roderigo Sanchez was a very high-ranking Mexican general who was found savagely beaten at his home in Ciudad Victoria. His murder investigation was the number one priority of the Mexican government in 2005. They suspected terrorists, cartels, or militants. They asked the US government to assist them with the investigation. We did. Our conclusion was that it was neither terrorist, cartels, nor militants. Those entities use bombs or at least guns, not frying pans and fireplace pokers."

"That was the murder weapon?" I asked.

"Well, it was hard to determine what 'weapon' actually killed the general. There were five household items that had the general's blood on them. It appeared to us that this was a crime of convenience committed by amateurs. There was nothing stolen from the home, so it wasn't a home invasion. There was no obvious motive. The case went very cold very quickly."

"So why ask these old college friends about the murder?" I asked.

"We don't know for sure, but Raymond did nothing on his 'vacation' but research his wife's friends. On Monday night, he began to research murders of Mexican generals during the week of March 28 to April 5, 2005. There was obviously only one, Roderigo Sanchez. We have no idea why he suspected these six friends of General Sanchez's murder, but it does make sense. Ben Eiler admitted that they were all in South Padre Island and drove into Mexico. Ciudad Victoria is only two hundred miles from Matamoras. The crime scene looked like it was created by scared college kids. It's very possible that Raymond White solved the biggest mystery in Mexico's history and then was killed for it."

CHAPTER 57

Agent Sylvia Batina

After dinner with Chief Denton, we walked back to the house on the island that the FBI had rented for me, Agent Mitchell, and Agent Bolding.

I turned to Agent Bolding and said, "Sir, I have some concerns about this investigation."

"Share them with me, Sylvia. I trust your judgment."

"Thank you, sir. I feel that we are treating this investigation differently than we would any other investigation because the victim was one of our own. Can you honestly say that, if anyone else had been very drunk on the deck of a ship during a thunderstorm late at night, we wouldn't have just chalked it up to a terrible accident and moved on?"

"Sylvia, I agree with you. We are treating this case very differently, and I am okay with that."

I said with a surprised voice, "You're okay with that?"

"Sylvia, you came from Bismark, North Dakota. In Bismark, you had to work Indian country. On a reservation, the FBI is the law. You had to work every case, from murder, rape, missing persons, theft, and white-collar crimes. You had no choice because, if you didn't work it, no one did. Working Indian country will either expose an agent as lazy and incompetent or highlight an agent for being able to manage a massive workload full of diverse cases. Sylvia, you shined in this role, and it was noticed, which is why you got promoted to the DC office. But we aren't in Bismark anymore. We don't have to work every case. We don't have the manpower to work every case. We must prioritize cases and neglect certain cases. I want any criminal to know, if you attack a member of the Justice Department 'family,' we will devote every resource we have and do whatever necessary to bring you to justice."

"I understand, Joshua—I mean, Agent Bolding, but what if Raymond White's death was an accident? What if these six friends are innocent. Is it fair to devote 'every resource we have and do whatever necessary' to harass and intimidate them so we can indict people who did nothing wrong?"

Agent Mitchell chimed in, "Sylvia, this conviction will give you the big win that you need to be promoted to management. You are a great agent. With this conviction, you could be promoted to special agent in charge, SAC, at a major office."

I responded, "I don't think I want to be promoted. I didn't join the FBI to play politics and climb the ranks. I joined the FBI to help people and protect our country. If this is what it takes to be management, maybe I am not cut out to be anything other than an agent."

There was silence for the next few steps.

As we were walking up the front doorsteps to our rental house, Agent Bolding said, "I heard a rumor that an attorney general once said that the FBI is bizarre. 'Only place I have seen where the best and brightest agents fight and cling to stay at their entry-level job.' I am not sure if that quote is true, but, Sylvia, you prove it to be accurate."

CHAPTER 58

Sophie Simmons

I'd never been involved in a political campaign before, but I felt like we needed to be in a crisis-management war room. The fate of our lives would depend on how we responded the next few days. I expressed these views to Jed, and he agreed. I loved it when he agreed with me. Was that wrong? Anyway, Jed asked me to gather everyone except Tommy and meet in the small saloon. I told him that I hated that room after it had been used as the interrogation room. I suggested that we meet on the back deck again. He smiled and agreed with me again.

After everyone was assembled on the back deck, there was silence. What happened? Nobody was talking to each other.

Finally I said, "Jed, what should we expect to happen next?"

Jed stood up. "Guys, it's going to get worse before it gets better. I don't think any of you had anything to do with Raymond's death, so we just keep telling the truth. Obviously they know something about Mexico, but I don't know how much. I do know that they don't have enough to arrest you all, or they would have already done it. So if you all give them no more additional information, they shouldn't be able to ever arrest you…unless there is evidence that comes forth from somewhere else. But it's been sixteen years, so while new evidence is possible, it's unlikely."

I was expecting questions from the group, but nobody looked up from their drinks.

Jed continued, "Without new evidence, they are going to need one of you to confess. They will target the one whom they see as the most vulnerable. Steve, I'm afraid that means that they will target you first. You are under federal indictment. They believe that you are desperate to cut a deal."

"Cut a deal? How would I help myself by admitting to being a part of killing a Mexican general?"

"You wouldn't, but they will hint of promises to you, hints of leniency. Remember, they're just 'hints.' There is no way that admitting to being part of a killing will help your situation. Regardless, know that they will target you."

Freedom stood up aggressively. "If they are targeting the weak, they should interrogate Theron again. He told the FBI that Weston and I didn't return to our room until 1:00 a.m. Thanks for that, Theron."

"That's true," said Theron defensively.

"It's not true. I think we returned to our cabin around twelve thirty, which we told the FBI, but why did you feel the need to rat us out?"

It was now Kelly's turn. "Speaking of ratting people out, someone told the FBI that I had visited Theron's room around 1:00 a.m. as well. Who did that?"

"Wait," Ben said. "Did you visit Theron's room at 1:00 a.m.?"

"I was going to the restroom, and Theron heard me. He thought it was Tommy sneaking some liquor and opened his cabin door. When he saw it was me, he invited me in to see how I was doing. Nothing happened, and I left a few minutes later. *That* is not the point, though. Why would one of you try to point the finger at me and Theron?"

"Stop!" Jed said loudly. "This is exactly what they want. They want you to turn on each other. This is their best hope in charging one of you, or all of you. Their investigation depends on you turning on each other."

There should not be this much tension on a beautiful boat anchored off the coast of a beautiful island, but there was. My friends of sixteen years didn't trust each other anymore.

In an attempt to remind everyone that we were in this together, I asked, "So what does the FBI know exactly?"

Ben spoke up, "They know that we were in South Padre Island during the week that the Mexican general died. They know that we crossed the border and went into Matamoras for a day. They obviously suspect that we went farther into Mexico and met the general, but I don't think they have proof of that."

I found it interesting that none of us would call the general by his name. We only called him the general. It was easier to deal with the guilt before we knew his name.

Ben was next to ask a question. "Jed, can the feds prosecute us for an alleged crime that was committed in Mexico?"

"Good question, Ben, and the answer is 'Not exactly.' They would have to extradite you all to Mexico to stand trial, or if they can convict you here in the States of another federal crime, any crime, even a charge like tax evasion"—I glanced at Weston and Freedom—"or insider trading"—I looked at Steve—"they can ask the judge to sentence you based on 'relevant conduct,' like you were convicted of murdering the Mexican general."

"Relevant conduct? What's that?" I asked.

"It allows a judge to sentence you for a crime that you have not plead guilty to nor has a jury convicted you of. A judge can even sentence you for conduct that a jury acquitted you of. Typically a prosecutor must prove to a jury of your peers beyond a reasonable doubt that you are guilty of the alleged crime. Relevant conduct requires a prosecutor at a sentencing hearing to only demonstrate to a judge that the preponderance of the evidence suggests that you, more likely than not, committed this additional alleged crime. So if any of you are convicted of any other federal crime, regardless of how small, you could be sentenced for murdering a Mexican general."

Jed's explanation wasn't very comforting. Steve looked as white as a ghost.

Kelly and Freedom were shell-shocked, and I couldn't help but cry.

Sweet Lauren was new to this secret and still had questions. "Jed, I don't understand. These friends were protecting a young girl from being raped. Where's the justice in going after these good people who had the courage to stop a monster from raping a young girl?"

"Lauren, if it's justice you seek, you will have to wait for it in heaven. In this world, you're stuck with the law."

CHAPTER 59

US Attorney Brian Banks

Saturday—

I had only been on the job for three weeks, and I already had a meeting this morning with DC agents who were going to ask me to empanel a grand jury to consider indicting six college friends for the murder of the deputy attorney general and a high-ranking Mexican general.

During my Senate confirmation, many members of the Senate judiciary were concerned that I had never been a prosecutor before. Hell, I had never been a practicing attorney before. After graduating law school first in my class, I clerked for a federal judge and then accepted a professorship at the University of North Carolina School of Law. I taught constitutional law and criminal law. I thought the fact that I was gay and in an openly gay marriage with Pete would be the most controversial topic during my confirmation hearing. I was wrong. Several senators were very concerned about my law review articles, where I discussed my view of our criminal justice system.

The basic premise of my view of the criminal justice system is that we have forsaken the notion of a "reluctant prosecutor." The prosecutor clearly plays a pivotal role in the administration of criminal justice. In our society, the prosecutor is often conferred the sole discretion to charge any person for any offense committed. Even if the responsibility to indict rests with a grand jury, the prosecutor knows that the grand jury will, in almost all circumstances, do whatever the prosecutor asks of them.

Obviously a prosecutor's decision to charge a person has great impact on the lives and liberty of the charged but also their families, their friends, and society at large. Therefore, this discretion should be exercised with extreme caution and after a deliberate and thorough process.

I would argue that the prosecutor's duty to the interests of justice, public interest, and professional ethics is significantly greater than the duty possessed by civil litigators. To understand this heightened duty that prosecutors possess, we must first determine who the prosecutor's client is. The answer to that question defines the role of the prosecutor. The prosecutor may list the state as the plaintiff in an action. But to be clear, the prosecutor should not represent the apparatus of government, nor does the prosecutor represent the victim. Instead his client should be society at large.

For society to be represented effectively, the accused, the court, and the community are entitled to expect that the prosecutor will perform his/her duties with fairness and detachment with the sole objective to achieve justice in accordance with the law and with a recognition of the limits of the law. For this reason, the prosecutor should eschew any notion of winning or losing a case. The prosecutor's role is not simply to protect society from violent offenders. The prosecutor's role is to seek and achieve justice and not merely to convict. A conviction and justice are not the same thing.

I didn't think these views were controversial, but several senators thought these views suggested that I might be "soft on crime." I was not soft on crime. I was just passionate about justice.

The career prosecutors in my office had warned me that DOJ attorneys and the FBI were also concerned that I would be a soft prosecutor. I was under great pressure to dispel this belief. Today would be my first exam.

"Good day. Thank you for coming to Raleigh. How was your trip from the island?"

After Agent Bolding told me of their travel difficulties (which weren't that difficult), we got down to business. They told me of their evidence against these six friends. I had a few questions.

"So the motive that you impose on these six friends is that one or more of them killed Raymond White because Mr. White had researched their personal and financial past and threatened them with criminal prosecution?"

"Yes," said Agent Bolding.

"Did Raymond White have a warrant to search these people's financial records and personal pasts?"

There was silence until Agent Betina spoke up, "No, he did not. We are not defending his behavior. He stepped way over the line."

"I would say so," I replied. "So Raymond's head had a contusion. The friends say that this contusion occurred on

Sunday night when, um, Sophie hit him on top of the head with a wine bottle to extract herself from his unwanted sexual advances, correct?"

"Yes."

"Can you determine when the contusion was made?"

Agent Betina fielded this question, "I'm afraid the saltwater that Raymond White's body floated in for several hours makes it impossible to make that determination. Truth be told, the saltwater makes it very difficult to even determine time of death. We are saying that he died around 1:00 a.m., but even that is very speculative."

"He was very drunk, and it was storming, so it is very possible that he did slip and fall over the boat."

"Yes, that is possible," said Agent Bolding.

"Okay, now to General Sanchez," I said. "You believe that Raymond suspected these friends of murdering the general, but you don't even know that for sure, do you?"

"We are quite confident that he had uncovered more information about these friends' involvement in General Sanchez's murder than we currently have."

"Why do you say that?" I asked.

"Well, we have confirmed that they were on a spring break trip to South Padre Island and crossed into Mexico, but Raymond had to have known something more specific, or he wouldn't have searched the death of a Mexican general during the week of March 28, 2005 to April 7, 2005. That is a very specific search. He had enough detailed evidence to be able to make such a specific search."

"I understand," I said, "but based on Raymond White's blatant disregard for these people's Fourth Amendment rights, I am going to need more than his suspicions. You need a confession or a witness. Is there anyone who could verify that these friends went to Ciudad Victoria, Mexico, or ever met this general?"

Agent Bolding responded, "We are working on a confession."

"But we can't even prosecute them for General Rodriguez's murder, right? We would have to extradite them to Mexico to stand trial," I asked.

"Not necessarily," said Agent Bolding. "It's true that we can't prosecute them for a crime committed in another country, but if we convicted one or more of them for any federal crime, including simply lying to a federal agent, we could use relevant conduct at the sentencing stage to sentence them as if they had been convicted for the murder of General Rodriguez," said Agent Bolding.

I did not respond. I was not a fan of relevant conduct.

Agent Bolding continued, "Mr. Banks, we realize that the case isn't that strong, but if we could get an indictment against even one of them, we believe that they will tell us everything. We just need to apply some pressure."

"Hmm," I sighed. "Based on the evidence that we have thus far, I don't know if a grand jury would indict them," I said.

"Mr. Banks, there's a reason that Judge Wachtler said, 'A grand jury would indict a ham sandwich if that's what a prosecutor wants.' The grand jury will do whatever we ask them to. Bring this to a grand jury. We will get an indictment, and then we can squeeze a confession out of at least one of them."

"Give me twenty-four hours to think about it," I said.

CHAPTER 60

Steve Camp

Sunday—

Jed was right. I was apparently seen as the "weak" one because Agent Bolding asked to interview me again today. I went to Jed and asked him for advice. He told me that the police questioning had gone from getting witness statements to a full-fledged murder investigation. He said that I should refuse to answer their questions without my lawyer present.

This time, they weren't coming onto the boat to interview me. They wanted me to meet them at the FBI's Wilmington Field Office. The office was a rather nondescript office building. The building was red bricked and two stories tall. The exterior and interior looked like it was designed in the 1970s. I had to surrender my cell phone as soon as I walked into the building. It was intimidating but not half as intimidating as when I walked into the conference room. As expected, there were agents Bolding, Betina, and Mitchell; but there were also eight other people in suits seated around a square table. My chair was seated in the middle, with all eight people staring at me.

Before they began their questioning of me, they introduced themselves. I couldn't remember any of their names, but there was an FBI agent from the Eastern District of New York. There was a United States attorney from the Eastern District of New York. There was a United States attorney from the Charlotte Office and several other people whose titles I missed, but I remember someone saying that they were "from main DOJ in Washington, DC."

Why were all these people here? What the hell was going on? I thought I was just meeting with Agent Bolding and maybe Chief Denton. How much had the government spent to fly all these people to Wilmington? This couldn't be good.

The FBI agents weren't doing the talking today.

US attorney Brian Banks began, "Mr. Camp, I know that you have answered a lot of questions over the last few days, but for the benefit of those of us who are new to the questioning, we would like to go over some things."

"Attorney Banks—I'm sorry. I don't know what I am supposed to call you."

"You can call me Mr. Banks."

"Okay, Mr. Banks, I'm sorry, but I have been instructed to tell you that I am not going to answer any more questions until I have a lawyer present."

Mr. Banks closed his notebook and said, "I understand."

The guy from "main DOJ" jumped in, "Mr. Camp, you have one opportunity to save yourself from a very long prison sentence, and that opportunity walks out the door when you do. This is your last chance. Either you tell us who killed Raymond White and why you all killed General

Rodriguez, or we are going to indict you in the Eastern District of North Carolina for conspiracy to commit murder. Good luck in trying to defend yourself in two federal trials at the same time. If you cooperate and tell us who killed Raymond and General Rodriguez, we can go easy on you."

"I have nothing to say until my lawyer is present."

The DC attorney replied, "Mr. Camp, we gave you the first bite at the apple, but if you don't take this deal, one of your friends will. Are you sure you want to throw away your only chance to benefit from your cooperation?"

"I have nothing to say until my lawyer is present."

"Do you really think your friends deserve your loyalty, a loyalty that I promise they won't reciprocate?"

"I have nothing to say until my lawyer is present."

"Okay, if you want to go, you're free to go. The next time I see you, you will be in an orange jumpsuit."

I was trembling like the island's beach grass blowing in the wind, but I managed to stand up and head for the door.

The DC lawyer said one last thing before I left, "Mr. Camp, I've known a lot of criminals, and the biggest regret they have in life is not for the wrong things they did but for the times they tried to do the right thing for the wrong people. Make sure your friends aren't the wrong people."

CHAPTER 61

Jed Cummins

Steve had asked me to drive him to the FBI office. We rented a car in Southport and drove the forty-five minutes to Wilmington. He asked me to be his attorney for the meeting, but I suggested that it would be better to have an excuse not to answer any more questions. Moreover, he already had a criminal defense attorney in New York with whom I didn't want to interfere with, and since both Sophie and Steve were involved in the Mexico incident, there was the distinct possibility of a conflict of interest.

Steve was nervous as he went into the meeting, but he was shaken as he came out. "Jed, they said they are going to indict me for conspiracy to murder Raymond White unless I told them who did. Can they really do that?"

I nodded. "Well, they were making threats to try to get you to turn on your friends. Their threats may be idle, but if they want an indictment, they can get an indictment. Grand juries are a joke. They were designed in England to be a citizen's shield against prosecutorial abuse, but they have turned out to be nothing but a sword that prosecutors use to squeeze people into cooperating or pleading guilty."

Steve was crying now. "Should I just tell them what they want to hear?"

"Steve, did you kill Raymond?"

"No, of course not."

"Do you know of anyone else who killed Raymond?"

"No."

"Do you want to confess to the killing of a Mexican general and hope that our justice system—or the Mexican government—believes you when you tell them that you were trying to prevent a rape?"

"No."

"Well, then you have only one option. You have to stay strong. Can you stay strong?"

"I think so. I've already endured so much since my indictment in New York I have gotten pretty good at staying strong."

CHAPTER 62

US Attorney Brian Banks

After refusing to answer our questions without his attorney present, Steve Camp left the interview room and the building. Now it was my turn to be the focus of the inquisition.

"Well, boss, what do you think?" asked Agent Mitchell. "You said that you wanted to see Steve Camp in person before you agreed to indict him. You saw him. He was nervous, flustered, sweating. He refused to answer any questions. An innocent person is willing to answer questions. An innocent person doesn't sweat when they are questioned."

"Oh, come on, Agent Mitchell," I replied. "You have been in the bureau too long if you think that innocent people don't get nervous when they are talking to a room full of federal agents and prosecutors. Anyone in their right mind would be visibly nervous."

Peter V. Noland III, Esq., was the name on his business card. I met him for the first time today. He was the new deputy attorney general, replacing Raymond White. I was immediately suspicious of any lawyer who referred to himself/herself as esquire on their business card. But he was the second highest-ranking lawyer in the Department of Justice, so I was determined to show him the deference that his office deserved.

Peter V. Noland III, Esq., was the next to speak. "Mr. Banks, tell us your thoughts on the matter."

"Well, I'm not convinced that he's guilty of murdering Raymond White."

"We wouldn't indict him for murder, only conspiring to commit murder," said Peter V. Noland III, Esq.

"I understand," I said. "I'm not sure any of them murdered Raymond White."

I was clearly the only one in the room who held that sentiment. Agent Mitchell threw up his hands in exasperation. Agent Bolding shook his head and looked at his feet. Mr. Noland turned around while shaking his head. There was a moment of silence until Mr. Noland turned back around to face me.

"Mr. Banks, let's look at the facts. First, while Raymond had been drinking on the night he went missing, he's been legally drunk every day for the past ten years that I've known him. I have never seen him so drunk that he would fall over a four-foot railing. I certainly have never seen him so drunk that he would allow himself to drown in warm water with a ladder to a boat only thirty feet away.

"Most of the suspects had motive to want Raymond dead. Almost all of them lied to the police chief. Raymond's wife lied about her being the beneficiary of Raymond's estate. She and Dr. Mason lied about not being romantically involved with each other. You don't spend the day with someone and then kiss them goodbye if you don't have feelings for that person. They also both lied when they said that they had stayed in their rooms alone all night.

"Steve Camp lied when he said that he had only talked to Jed Cummins about his pending divorce. He lied when he didn't tell the chief that he was a parolee awaiting trial and had violated the terms of his parole by being on that boat.

"Weston Walker and Freedom Goforth were very suspicious when telling us what they had been doing that night. They claimed that they went skinny-dipping. Who does that in the middle of the night? They couldn't tell us when they came inside. Did they tell us they went skinny-dipping to have an explanation ready if someone saw them in the water drowning Raymond? They also lied about the privileged conversations they had with Jed Cummins.

"Ben Eiler lied about how he got his job with Coca-Cola. He lied about his conversation with Jed Cummins. Sophie Simmons had already tried to kill him once when she smashed a wine bottle over his head on Sunday night. The only reason she didn't lie was because she had her boyfriend acting as her attorney and only answered a few questions. I don't know which one of them killed Raymond or if they did it all together, kind of a *Murder on the Orient Express* scenario. But one of them murdered Raymond, and Steve Camp knows who did it…and we haven't even begun to talk about General Rodriguez."

Peter V. Noland III, Esq., made a compelling closing argument.

My initial response was "I'm not sure that we can say that they lied. They just didn't tell the whole truth."

"Is there a difference?" asked Agent Mitchell.

"Yes, there is a legal difference, but I will agree that they were trying to hide something or maybe several things."

I started pacing the room as I gathered my thoughts. This job was harder than I had imagined. The president of the United States appointed *me* to make these decisions, not Agent Bolding, not Agent Mitchell, not even Peter V. Noland III, Esq. The president trusted my instincts, my sense of fairness, and my sense of justice. I didn't think there was enough evidence to indict anyone yet, but the pressure coming from the career prosecutors and FBI agents was intense. I was going to have to work with these people for years. How effective would I be if my first big decision was viewed by my "team" as weak?

"What happens if we indict Steve Camp and then discover that he had nothing to do with Raymond White's murder?" I asked.

"First we probably find out that Steve Camp wasn't involved after he cooperates and tells us who did murder Raymond," replied Peter V. Noland III, Esq. "If Mr. Camp convinces us that he was not involved with Raymond's death, we will amend the indictment to remove the conspiracy charge and then offer him leniency on his insider trading charges. If you think about it, we are really doing Mr. Camp a favor by giving him the first chance to snitch on his friends and be treated with leniency on his existing charges."

I continued to gather my thoughts and then said, "Okay, go get an indictment charging Steve Camp with conspiracy in the murder of Raymond White."

CHAPTER 63

Dr. Theron Mason

While Jed drove Steve to his meeting at the FBI, the rest of us paced around the boat nervously. Since we were docked at the marina, the girls decided to go to the Island Retreat and Spa to ease their tension. Weston, Ben, and I decided to go for a jog through the maritime forest to sweat out the stress. When we returned from our run, Jed and Steve were already at the boat. Steve and the FBI must have had a short meeting.

Steve had retreated to his room, so Jed told us about Steve's reaction to the meeting. We felt sorry for Steve. All of us had endured a lot this week, but Steve had endured abundantly more than the rest of us—apart from perhaps Kelly.

While Steve was in his room, the rest of us whispered questions to Jed.

It started with Sophie. "Jed, do you really think the feds will charge him with Raymond's death?"

"Sophie, I wouldn't think so. There's just not enough evidence. The only thing a prosecutor wants more than a conviction is to avoid losing a high-profile case. The trial of the deputy attorney general's alleged killer will be high profile. On the other hand, they don't like to make idle threats. If they develop a reputation for bluffing, then their future threats won't be taken serious by defense counsel."

"Would they really give him leniency if he lied and told them that one of us killed Raymond?" asked Weston.

"Absolutely," said Jed. "It's a major weakness in our system. It's a crime for anyone to bribe or even influence a witness, but Congress carved out an exception for prosecutors. They can offer immunity, leniency, even money in some circumstances for witnesses who are willing to say what they want them to say. They also will threaten additional charges, prison time, or even the prosecution of the person's family members if they refuse to cooperate. Our modern method of incentivizing defendants to testify against other defendants are termed contingent agreements. These offers of leniency are conditioned upon the prosecutor's evaluation of the value of the witness's cooperation in prosecuting other defendants. Notice the measurement of cooperation is not that the cooperating witness told the truth. The measurement of cooperation is its value in obtaining a conviction."

"That is terrible," I said. "How is their testimony reliable if the witness is being bribed or threatened by the prosecutors?"

"No reasonable person who understands how the world works would consider it reliable testimony. Congress isn't known for exercising reason, though, when it comes to responding to the Justice Department. Congress does whatever the Justice Department wants because they are afraid of being labeled soft on crime."

"This is very depressing," said Freedom.

"I know," Jed said.

Sophie interjected some wisdom, "Guys, I think we all need a night of happiness, especially Steve. Let's talk about something else."

I had an idea. At the beginning of the week, I had made dinner reservations for tonight at Shoals Club. With all the crises that had occurred during the week, we had never ventured onto the island to eat. Why not try to take our minds off things with a nice dinner and some great wine? Jed loved the idea—as long as we could conclude the evening with a postdinner cigar.

When we told the girls, their faces lit up. I think we all needed a reminder of what normal life was like. The girls put makeup on for the first time in several days. They put on cocktail dresses and looked as good as they did at the beginning of the week. It delighted me to watch Kelly smile and laugh. She seemed happier than she had been all week.

I knocked on Steve's cabin door. He acknowledged my knock but didn't open the door. I told him of our plans through the door, and he said that he would join us. He came out looking dapper with a plaid sports coat, linen pants, and loafers with no socks. Maybe tonight would allow us to salvage something from this otherwise horrific week.

The Shoals Club was everything you could hope it to be. The Aqua Coastal Cuisine was the club's premier dining venue. The food was exquisite but couldn't compete with the stunning ocean views.

Steve appreciated our commitment to not talk about the day's meeting, so we obliged him and instead told of old stories from our college days. The highlight of the evening came when Steve stood up to make a toast.

He quoted from Queen's "We Are the Champions," "I've paid my dues, time after time. I've done my sentence but committed no crime, and bad mistakes, I've made a few. I've had my share of sand kicked in my face. But I've come through."

CHAPTER 64

Ben Eiler

The cigars were stronger than I was used to. We had returned to the boat, but since Theron had drunk several glasses of wine at dinner, we decided to keep the boat at the marina for tonight. The view from the marina was not as picturesque as being anchored a half mile off the coast, but the marina did have a fun vibe. There were several boats docked in the marina. People were grilling out, listening to music, and enjoying each other's company.

As we sat on the back deck smoking cigars, Kelly checked her emails. "You've got to be kidding me," she said.

"What is it?" Theron asked.

"My lawyer just emailed me. Raymond did not have a will. I inherit everything. How could that asshole not have a will? He was the second most powerful lawyer in the country."

"Isn't that a good thing?" Lauren asked.

"No," Jed replied. "She just inherited a million more motives."

"I guess I will be the next one to get Steve's treatment," said Kelly. Kelly began to cry. "Why did this have to happen?"

Theron walked across the deck toward Kelly, sat down next to her, and put his arm around her. "We are going to get through this. I promise," Theron assured Kelly.

"Well, hello, everyone. What brings you all to the marina?" It was Chief Denton walking by carrying a coffee cup from Sandpiper Coffee and Cream.

"Chief," said Jed with surprise in his voice. "What are you doing at the marina? It's kind of late for coffee, isn't it?"

"It's never too late for coffee," he replied with a chuckle.

"Well, it may be too late to question us tonight," said Jed.

The chief put up his hands in an I-surrender posture. "I'm not going to be questioning you tonight or any other time. The feds took over the case and basically said that we weren't needed. So until I hear otherwise, my office has closed this file."

"Chief, you told us we had to stay on the island until you gave us permission to leave. If you have closed your file, does that mean we can leave?" asked Theron.

"If the feds want you to stay, they can tell you to stay. As I said, I've closed my file, so I can't force you to stay on the island."

"I wish you were still involved in the case. I trust you a lot more than I do the feds," replied Jed.

"You shouldn't trust me. The last thing I told the feds was that it was my belief that one or all of you murdered Raymond White...but I can't prove it. I hope they can."

CHAPTER 65

Sophie Simmons

Monday—

What a glorious morning! After waking up at sea for a week, it was nice to wake up to the sounds of a bustling community. The ferries, which were appropriately named *Revenge* and *Adventure*—both named after ships from Blackbeard's infamous fleet—were coming into the marina. Tourists and workers were unloading, excited about another day on the sun-drenched island. The seagulls were circling as they looked for their breakfast. Jed and I had slept in due to the late night of drinking. As I got my coffee, it appeared that we weren't the only ones who had slept in. Nobody else was awake either. The boat was as empty as Jesus's tomb on the third day.

"Good morning, Sophie." It was Kelly.

"How are you feeling this morning?" I asked.

"I'm terrified, I went to bed feeling defeated, but I woke up this morning feeling determined. We didn't do anything wrong, and I am determined to prove that we didn't."

I hugged Kelly and said, "You arrived on this boat a timid and scared woman, but despite everything, you are leaving a determined and courageous widow. I am so proud of you."

"I smell bacon," said Freedom.

"Yes, Tommy is making us breakfast this morning," I said. "He designed a menu of biscuits, bacon, and cheese. Not very healthy, but it is sweet of him to cook for us. While we wait for his delicious concoction, would you like some freshly made coffee courtesy of Chef Sophie?" I joked.

We girls laughed like we were back in college. It felt good to be with my old friends again.

"What's so funny?" said Jed.

He was accompanied by Ben and Lauren.

"Do you really want to know?" I asked. "We may have been laughing at you behind your back." I winked at him and gave him a kiss as I poured him a cup of coffee.

Theron came down from the bridge. "Good morning," he said. "It is so hot today. From the bridge, I could see trees trying to bribe the dogs."

We laughed and enjoyed each other's company as we watched the tourists arrive for a new week of island adventures. The island reminded me of my time as a summer camp counselor. The counselors were there all summer. At the end of each week, we counselors would be exhausted; but come Saturday afternoon, a new crop of campers would arrive with such contagious energy and excitement we counselors couldn't help but be infected with their enthusiasm. Likewise, the daily arrival of excited vacationers to the island provided the locals the same infectious energy that I had experienced as a counselor.

Today was going to be our last day on the boat. Since the sheriff had told us last night that we could go home and the feds had never commanded us to stick around, we decided that we would all head home and have a daily Zoom call to give updates and discuss strategy until this nightmare was over.

Tommy and Theron were preparing the boat to be sailed back to Myrtle Beach, and everyone else was packing up their luggage.

"Has anyone seen Steve this morning?" I asked.

"No," said Freedom.

"I haven't," said Lauren.

I wanted to let him sleep in, but I also wanted to make sure that he had enough time to say his goodbyes.

"Steve?" I said as I knocked on his door.

There was no answer.

"Steve," I said a little louder.

Still no response.

I opened his cabin door. His luggage was packed, but he wasn't in his room. I started to go find him on the boat when I saw a letter on his bed.

> I am so sorry. I can't take it anymore. For the most part, I am proud of the life that I have led. I have tried to be a good friend, a good husband, and a good father. I worked hard and played by the rules. I never intentionally hurt anyone, and if I did, please accept my apology. I don't believe that I ever traded on insider information, but I did kill Raymond White. I didn't do it intentionally; but I, and I alone, am responsible for his death.

That night, I went to the deck to ask Raymond why he was trying to destroy everyone's life. I had no illusions of changing his mind, but I at least wanted to understand what motivated him to be so cruel to his lovely wife and to her friends, whom he had only met a few days ago. His answers to my questions were not satisfying, so I kept probing. I guess I pressed him too hard. He got in my face and told me that he couldn't wait to see me become a prison bitch. I shoved him away from me. He took a swing at me but was too drunk to connect with his punch. I dodged his punch and then came back with one of my own. I didn't miss. I hit him with an uppercut square on the nose, sending him backward over the boat's railings. I looked over the railing and saw that he was lying lifeless in the water. I didn't try to rescue him or notify anyone. Instead I returned to my cabin, where I unsuccessfully attempted to go to sleep. I am solely responsible for Raymond's death. My friends had nothing to do with it and are learning of my involvement for the first time as they read this letter. To them, I apologize for putting them through the last week. To Kelly, I am sorry for accidentally killing your husband.

To my two sons, Cooper and Blake, the men that will carry on the Camp family name, I am so sorry to have caused you pain. I wish so desperately that things would have been different. I will miss you two so very much; but I hope, after a few months, my actions this morning will have made your lives easier.

I want you each to know that you have exceeded my wildest expectations, not because you are perfect because no one is. You make mistakes, and you will make more as you get older. But you both have good hearts. I am so proud to have been your dad.

Since I won't be there as you reach milestones on your path to manhood, I would like to share with you some advice—some of which I've learned from my own mistakes and some which I've learned because I did it the right way and reaped the benefits:

1) Choose to be kinder than you need to be.
2) You show the world who you are by the way you do the small tasks. There is never a job too small.
3) Work hard. There's nothing more rewarding to a man than putting

in a hard day's work. Embrace work. Don't shy away from it.

4) Be a forgiving friend. You will encounter people in your life who will let you down or even hurt you. There is nothing more life-giving than forgiveness. It deepens relationships and honors God. It also blesses you. It blesses you with a happy heart and appreciative people in your life and allows you to live free. Be quick to forgive and slow to judge.

5) Have fun. Life is an adventure that is meant to be lived. Do not allow fear or trepidation prevent you from experiencing life to its fullest. If your desires are good and wholesome, embrace your desires. Pursue them with reckless abandon. Don't let other people or your own fears prevent you from pursuing your goals. Be adventurous. Be a risk taker. Be a warrior.

6) Embrace manhood. Being a man is a lot of responsibility. You are often expected to be the provider, the protector, the hunter,

the builder, and the warrior. These are very rough-and-tumble roles that God has given to us men, and it's what makes us men. It's why your heart races and you get excited when you watch a war movie or a battle on the football field. It's what devastates you when you lose a contest. These are God-given traits that he writes on the heart of every man, and they are the impulses that drive men to achieve great things. Embrace this role and cultivate it. However, the test of a real man is to embrace your masculinity while still being compassionate, tender, loving, and a seeker of peace. This is a difficult balance to maintain, but you both are off to a great start.

7) Love justice. This may seem strange coming from me, but what I have experienced over the last several years is due to a system of justice. But it's not justice. Justice is seeking to lift those who are downtrodden, seeking to protect those who are in danger, seeking to comfort those who are

in fear, and seeking to right those who have been wronged. Great achievements have occurred throughout history by men who love justice and fairness.

8) Embrace failure. Failure only occurs to men who have tried. There is no shame in failure. The only shame that exists is when you allow failure to defeat you. Failure is the greatest teacher in life. If viewed properly, it is a necessary stepping-stone to achievement. For every failure (personal, athletic, or professional), realize that you are one step closer to achieving your goals.

These are just a few of the lessons that I learned throughout my abbreviated life. I am so extremely proud of each of you and excited for what the future holds for you. I wish I could be there to watch both of you live life well. Take care of your mother. Always protect her and love her.

Know this: you will always have a dad who was proud of you, who loved you more than life itself, and whose spirit will be there with you to celebrate your achievements and love you in your failures.

With apologies to those who I have wronged, gratitude for those who I have loved, and with malice toward none, goodbye.

Steve Camp

CHAPTER 66

Freedom Goforth

"Steve, where are you? Don't do it, Steve…Please, Steve."

The boat was pandemonium. We were all desperate to find Steve before he did something terrible. We were running through the boat, checking every room. Theron was scouring the marina boardwalks with his binoculars looking for Steve.

Ben came running into the hallway. "Guys, I went to my cabin to look in my bag. I had my Colt .45 in the bag, and now it's gone."

"Oh my god," I said. "How did he know there was a gun in your bag?" I asked.

"Well, I showed it to him," said Ben. "We were talking about how he had to surrender his guns once he was indicted. I asked him what kind of guns he had. One thing led to another, and I took him to my cabin to show him my new pistol."

"He's got to be on the island. Everyone, take a different golf cart and look for him. I'll call the Chief," said Theron.

Jed and Sophie headed to Cape Fear. Theron and Kelly went to the market, and Weston and I took off for Old Baldy. Even Tommy, who had taken a liking to Steve, started searching for him by foot.

I desperately wanted to find my friend, but at the same time, I did not want to be the one who found him if he had done the unthinkable. It turned out that Weston and I had drawn the short straw. After searching around the lighthouse to no avail, Weston began to race past the chapel on the way to the turtle conservancy.

"Weston," I said as I began to weep, "stop the golf cart. We found him, and it's too late."

CHAPTER 67

US Attorney Brian Banks

I sat down at my desk and tried not to let a tear escape. I couldn't believe that Steve Camp had committed suicide. Did I drive him to it? Of course, I did. This job was not what I expected. I was beginning to miss the days at Chapel Hill when my most trying decision was whether to give a student a failing grade or let him pass with a D minus. They told me that, if we indicted him, he would confess. I never thought he would kill himself.

That letter he wrote, the message he sent to his boys, my God, I couldn't stop crying as they read the letter to me. He may have killed Raymond White, but it sounded like Steve Camp was a much better man than Raymond White was. I was reconsidering my future at the US Attorney's Office when Agent Bolding and his team knocked on my door.

"Come in," I said.

I guess they could see that I was shaken up about the news of Steve Camp's suicide.

"Hey, boss, tough day, huh?"

"Yeah, you could say that," I replied.

"It's never good when the culprit takes their own life, but it often happens when people are facing extended prison time. I hate to say that you will get used to it, but you will get used to it."

I looked at Agent Bowling and said, "I don't want to get used to it."

Agent Betina spoke with more sympathy, "Mr. Banks, I understand. I will never get used to it myself, but we must remember that it was Steve Camp's actions that caused this terrible chain of events to occur. Steve Camp's actions resulted in the death of Raymond White. Steve Camp is the one who took his own life, and it was Steve Camp's actions that resulted in his two boys growing up without a father."

It was now Agent Mitchell's turn to assuage my nagging regret. "We got the bad guy, boss. Not in the way that we would have desired, but we got the bad guy."

I know they were trying to make me feel better, but it wasn't helping. So I changed the subject.

"So when are you all going back to DC?"

"Well, don't we still have the murder of General Sanchez to investigate?"

I was shocked. I stood up from my desk. "The murder of General Sanchez? Are you kidding me? There is zero evidence beyond Raymond White's Google search that these people had anything to do with the murder of a Mexican general. I am not going to persecute these people anymore. Mexico can investigate General Sanchez's murder if they want. I, for one, am done."

"Okay, we just wanted to check with you," said Agent Bolding. "I guess we will be going back to DC today then."

"Safe travels," I said to them as I ushered them out of my office.

Agent Bolding shook my hand and commented, "It was nice working with you, Mr. Banks."

"You too. Thank you for your help," I responded though I didn't mean it.

CHAPTER 68

Sophie Cummins

I couldn't believe that we were having another reunion at Bald Head Island. With all the tragedy that occurred on the island last year, I thought that I would never come back. However, after Steve's suicide, the island folks showed incredible kindness and hospitality to us. Chief Denton was very sympathetic and treated Steve's body like it was a family member. The mayor of the island and his wife invited us to their home for dinner and drinks. They opened the chapel to us so we could have a small celebration of Steve's life before we left the island. In attendance was Chief Denton, the mayor, and scores of other islanders who had never met Steve but came to offer us support.

We asked the mayor if it would be possible for us to place a tribute of Steve near the chapel where he died. The mayor agreed. It had been one year since Steve's death, and we were all returning to Bald Head Island to place the stone with commemorative placard next to the chapel. Theron designed the three-foot stone with the gold placard. The placard read:

May all who read this strive to lead a
life as well as our friend, Steve Camp, did.

He was a loving father and a loyal friend.

Beneath this inscription, the following was etched into the placard in Steve's own handwriting:

With apologies to those who I have wronged, gratitude for those who I have loved, and with malice toward none, goodbye.

Steve Camp

It was a lovely tribute to a lovely man. Theron also established a trust for Cooper and Blake Camp. It was a trust that would pay for them to attend summer camp every year, pay for the boys and their mother to take a vacation once a year, and then pay for their college tuition at any school that they wanted to attend. Whatever money was left over would be split between the two boys when they had both graduated college. The first vacation that the boys wanted to take was to Bald Head Island to be a part of the dedication of their father's placard. Their mother graciously agreed. We couldn't wait to see them again.

In the last year, Jed and I got married. I hadn't told Freedom or Kelly yet; but I had other news as well. I was thirteen weeks pregnant. I planned on telling them during this trip. We only lived a few hours from Ben and Lauren and had become very good friends with them. We had gotten to know their eight precious children and absolutely adored them.

We drove with Ben and Lauren to Southport to await the arrival of Theron's new boat—just too many memories on the *Nomism's*. He traded it in and supposedly downsized to a twenty-million-dollar yacht. When we arrived at the marina, Wes and Freedom were already there. That was not like Freedom to be early. I hoped everything was okay. After a few minutes of catching up, our concerns were allayed. They were doing great. After Netflix rejected Wes's last production, HBO bought it. Freedom was finally a movie star and had several more projects in the works.

The horn sounded as Theron's new boat entered the marina. Kelly was on the front deck waving at us. Theron and Kelly spent several months dating, with Theron travelling to DC on most weekends to help Kelly probate Raymond's estate and sell her Georgetown brownstone. About five months ago, Kelly moved to Greenville and had enrolled in law school this coming fall. Life had moved on, and it didn't seem fair. Anyone of us could have done the same thing that Steve did. Hell, I hit Raymond with a wine bottle; but for the grace of God, Raymond could have fallen over the railing on Sunday night.

Steve deserved better out of this life. The world would be a better place if Steve were still in it. I have heard it said, "It is a fortunate man who finds one true friend in his lifetime." Steve's life may have ended prematurely, but he lived a very fortunate life because he had not only one true friend but five true friends who loved him dearly and would live the remainder of their lives in such a way as to honor the memory of our friend, Steve Camp.

CHAPTER 69

Brian Banks

It had been a long year. I resigned my office as US attorney two weeks after Steve Camp's death. Despite everyone at the office and Department of Justice complimenting me on a successful outcome, I never felt at peace with the way that Steve Camp's case had been handled. I often lay awake at night replaying every decision that I made in that case. It could have been handled in a hundred different ways; and ninety-nine of those ways would result in Steve Camp being alive, maybe in prison, but alive. Steve Camp was not a cold-blooded killer. After two weeks, I realized that I did not want to be a part of a system that offers congratulations when a man like Steve Camp takes his own life.

I had resumed my teaching duties at the law school. I had joined several organizations that were pushing for criminal justice reform. Most days, I was happy, but not today. Today was the one-year anniversary of Steve Camp's death. To put it mildly, I was feeling melancholy. I was in my home office with a glass of Four Roses Bourbon and listening to my favorite Nina Simone album.

I opened a desk drawer and pulled out a copy of Steve's suicide letter. I had read it a couple of times in the last year, and each time, my stomach twisted into a knot. It was not pleasant, but it was a helpful reminder of—wait. I read the same passage from Steve's letter over again. Where was the Steve Camp file? I turned on my laptop and searched for his file. There it was. How could this be? The coroner's report stated that there was only one contusion, and it was on top of Raymond White's head. Sophie Simmons claimed that she caused that contusion on Sunday night when she hit Raymond over the top of his head with a wine bottle, but Steve's letter said:

> He took a swing at me but was too drunk to connect with his punch. I dodged his punch and then came back with one of my own. I didn't miss. I hit him with an uppercut square on the nose, sending him backward over the boat's railings.

The coroner's report showed no signs that Raymond White had been punched in the nose—or anywhere else on the face. Why would Steve Camp lie in his last statement? Why would he say that he hit Raymond White in the nose when he didn't, when he couldn't have? Was he protecting the real killer? Was there even a killer, or had Raymond White fallen over the railing while in a drunken stupor like the friends claimed? Did Steve Camp break under the pressure that I was applying and decide in his last act to accept blame for a crime that he didn't commit to protect his friends from the same type of pressure that I had applied to him?

Oh my god, what had I done? Steve Camp didn't kill Raymond White. As I sat there wondering what I should do with this information, it occurred to me I was not an agent of the Department of Justice. I had no duty to do anything with this revelation. If anything, I owed Steve Camp a duty to honor his last wish—which was to protect his friends from prosecutors like me.

I deleted Steve Camp's file on my computer, poured myself another glass of Four Roses, turned up the volume on Nina Simone, and lifted my glass. "To you, Steve Camp, your secret is safe with me."

-The End-

About Bald Head Island

This story isn't complete without also telling you about the history, charm, and darkness of Bald Head Island. In a story full of fascinating characters, Bald Head Island distinguished itself as the protagonist of our story.

Bald Head Island is a unique coastal island located in North Carolina at the intersection of the Cape Fear River and the Atlantic Ocean. It rests just south of the Outer Banks. It got its name from the dunes on its South Beach becoming worn down to the point of resembling a bald head. Before lighthouses, mariners would navigate into the river looking for the "bald head" to navigate them.

At the easternmost point of Bald Head Island lies Cape Fear. Cape Fear received its name due to the dangerous shoals that shipwrecked countless unwitting sailors.

Due to the countless shipwrecks which occurred off Bald Head, in 1817, Thomas Jefferson commissioned a lighthouse to be built on the island. The lighthouse is still the only high-rise on the island and is affectionately known as Old Baldy. You can still climb the 108 stairs inside Old Baldy for a spectacular panoramic view of the island.

Today Bald Head Island is a resort community accessible only by ferry or private boat and where no cars are allowed. Of the Island's twelve thousand acres, ten thousand acres consist of beach, salt marsh, and maritime forest, which are protected and will remain undeveloped. The island is home to only 220 permanent residents; but the island's summer population swells to approximately 3,000 weekly residents who rent one of the 1,120 beautiful homes for a week of relaxation, golf, surfing, biking, kayaking, fishing, etc.

The fact that golf carts and bicycles are the only means of transportation adds to the charm of the island. During the day, the sand dunes, salt marshes, Spanish moss, palm trees, live oaks, alligators, white-tailed deer, and a protected sea turtle population make it an outdoor paradise. However, at night, the darkness of the island is all-encompassing. Because the vast of majority of the island is protected from development, all commercial activity shuts down at 8:00 p.m., and there are no lights or sounds that are generated from vehicle traffic. The nights on Bald Head Island are pitch black, with only the sounds of the waves lapping against the beaches, the sounds of wildlife, and the sound of wind—which is never ending.

Bald Head Island has not always been so idyllic. In the seventeenth and eighteenth centuries, when pirates ruled the waters off the coast of North Carolina with greed and terror, Bald Head Island was a favorite refuge and base for these notorious buccaneers. The waters surrounding Cape Fear were a hideaway for hundreds of pirates, the most famous of which was Edward Teach, better known as Blackbeard.

In a nod to this colorful past, the island hosts an annual festival called Pirate Invasion. Additionally, today's visitors are transported to the island aboard ferries appropriately named *Revenge* and *Adventure*—both ships from Blackbeard's infamous fleet.

ABOUT THE AUTHOR

Jeremy Hutchinson was a deputy prosecuting attorney and a partner in a successful law firm. He was elected to the Arkansas House of Representatives in 2001 and the Arkansas State Senate in 2010. Jeremy Hutchinson served as chairman of the Senate Judiciary Committee.

He served in the Senate until 2018, when he was indicted for federal white-collar crimes. With his experience as a prosecutor and a defendant, Jeremy Hutchinson has a deep understanding of the criminal justice system, both the good and the bad.

Jeremy Hutchinson volunteers with prison reentry and drug-rehabilitation ministries.

Jeremy Hutchinson is married and has three children and two stepchildren. Jeremy and his family have vacationed at Bald Head Island for many years and has grown to love the island and its people.

9 781684 986101